A NAVAL ENGAGEMENT

Surgeon Commander Alexander Carlton Roscoe RN does absolutely nothing for her pulse or her blood pressure, Sister Kitty Martin insists. Yet why does the very thought of the dynamic surgeon, who is also a wounded war hero, make her heart beat faster?

A NAVAL ENGAGEMENT

BY

ELSPETH O'BRIEN

MILLS & BOON LIMITED
London · Sydney · Toronto

First published in Great Britain 1984
by Mills & Boon Limited, 15–16 Brook's Mews,
London W1A 1DR

© Elspeth O'Brien 1984

Australian copyright 1984
Philippine copyright 1984

ISBN 0 263 74647 X

Set in 11 on 12½ pt Linotron Times
03–0484–46,000

Photoset by Rowland Phototypesetting Ltd
Bury St Edmunds, Suffolk
Made and printed in Great Britain by
Richard Clay (The Chaucer Press) Ltd
Bungay, Suffolk

CHAPTER ONE

SISTER Kitty Martin picked up the small white card and read the address. She raised her eyebrows, 'I thought the panic was over and they hoped to close down for running repairs and redecorating.' She tapped her cheek with the edge of the card and her deep blue eyes were serious.

Miss Rankin, the head of the nursing agency near Newport on the Isle of Wight, looked anxious.

'You don't object to another week or so there?' she said. 'It won't be as interesting or as busy, but I'm sure that the three men there must have something to interest you, professionally if nothing more. They especially asked for someone who had been there after the Falklands war, who might even remember the men who are coming back for a while.'

'Not at all. I liked it there and the work was very satisfying,' Kitty said. She thought back to the day when she had first reported for duty at the Convalescent Home for Officers in the old staff quarters of Osborne House, the Victorian mansion in which Queen Victoria had spent some of the happiest times of her life, with her large family. On that day, the men had seemed different from the kind of

5

patient she was used to nursing. All were intelligent, some high-ranking, but somewhere in their eyes was a cloud of remembered suffering and shock, as if something had happened in which they could not believe entirely, something that happened to other men on news programmes, and not to them.

'Do you know who has come back?' she asked.

'No idea, I'm afraid. You will be the most experienced nursing sister there and the secretary wasn't very forthcoming with details. Most of the senior staff are on leave, but there will be one nurse on night duty and a nursing auxiliary, and you to cover days. A physio girl will come in on a part-time basis. The head of nursing and the House Governor normally running the place is away for a while. His replacement will be a local doctor, also RN retired, who will keep an eye on things, but the work will be light and as you make it.'

Kitty Martin tried to think back to the worst cases among the wounded fresh from surgical or medical treatment after the ordeal of war. Some men had come for only a few days before going on leave, but others with deeper wounds of mind or body had been sent back to hospital for further treatment.

'Captain Oliver said he would like to come back while he got used to his prosthesis. He lost a foot when a mine blew up when he tried to de-fuse it.' She sighed. 'It didn't seem fair. He is almost due to retire from the Parachute regiment and this happened on the day that he was leaving the Falklands.'

'Well, whoever is there, they'll be glad to see you. Can you make it this evening? Just to get some idea of drugs and treatment so that if you need to put in a chitty, you can have delivery tomorrow.'

'Yes, I can go there now,' said Sister Martin, making a mental note to fetch her clean uniform from the houseboat that was her home on the banks of Wootton Creek, a convenient address from whence she could travel to whatever job was offered her by the agency. She tucked the card away safely, as proof of her official status when she had to pass the lodge gates of Osborne House on her way to the convalescent home.

Her small moped puffed as it turned from the main road to go between the huge and very impressive wrought-iron gates. She looked with pleasure at the well-kept lawns and beautiful terraces that flanked the Italianate buildings. The attendant in the lodge smiled and waved her along the drive, recognising her as the young nursing sister who had put in so many hours when the first batch of wounded from the Falklands had come to Osborne to rest after treatment, and to recover poise and confidence. Not since World War II had the old place been so stirred. Convalescents came and went all the time after accidents and wounds acquired in Northern Ireland and on manoeuvres, but not in such numbers as from the Southern Ocean war.

The put-put of the moped seemed incongruous in

a park more geared to horses and the memories of Victoria's carriages, but familiarity with the place took away the sense of awe that Kitty had felt when first she came along this drive. She parked neatly at the side of the staff car park and walked with her crash helmet under one arm to the entrance. The fresh spring breeze caught her hair, tossing it over her eyes and making her stop to push the thick brown strands back as she entered the sheltered hall.

It was all so familiar and restful. After a training in a busy general hospital on the mainland, followed by a few months in the acute surgery unit of the Birmingham Accident Hospital, this was another world. The gentle slopes of the lawn under the huge spreading cedar tree spoke of elegance and leisure and a style of living no longer seen in modern times. But this was a haven, as she knew from her previous work here, and the surroundings were perhaps more valuable to wounded bodies and minds than all the skilled therapy available in the various departments of the convalescent home.

She reported to the office and was in time to catch the secretary before she left for the night.

'I thought the place would be empty,' Kitty said.

'Never quite empty and we have been very busy until last month when there was a sudden exodus. It was then that certain rooms that really needed attention were scheduled for repairs and refurbishing and some of the staff took holidays that they had postponed during the busy time. We have several men from army units who have relatives staying in the visitors' guest house in the grounds. Most of them are almost self-sufficient and wander about playing golf and strolling down to the beach when the weather is as still as it is today. Once they have done their remedial exercises or had physio, they are free to enjoy the facilities here.'

'Are there any who really need nursing?'

'The three men who came back and are the last of the Falklands batch. Captain Oliver from Para 2 who lost a foot is here for more physio and the opportunity to use his new foot without half his friends watching him.' Kitty nodded. 'Then there is Lt Commander Sinclair who was badly burned when his ship was hit and was picked up from the sea half dead.'

'I didn't meet him,' said Sister Martin.

'No, he wasn't here for more than a week at a time between grafts and I think you were away each time. He's quite fun when he forgets about his condition but it must be depressing for a good-looking young man to think that he is less than he was.' She frowned. 'He seems fine now, but he'll be glad of a bright face and needs a little judicious bullying.'

'Only two?'

'No, the third man who needs cheering up is rather difficult. He doesn't respond well and has something on his mind.' She sighed. 'Nice, but such a chip on his shoulder. An army man, or rather marine, called Captain Bruce Mycroft.' She sighed.

'He doesn't get on with our locum surgeon at all.'

'Who came to relieve the holiday rosta?' Kitty asked.

'You may recall a former patient called Roscoe? Surgeon Commander Alexander Carlton Roscoe?'

'You don't sound too keen. Now let me see. I think I saw him once when he was here after the removal of a piece of metal from his back. He was sitting down at the time and I had nothing to do with his treatment.'

'Well, the notes are all here so I advise you to mug up on them before you see the Commander.' Kitty looked puzzled, so she went on, 'When he was here, we all liked him. I might even say that most of the staff swooned when he appeared, but he has changed. I spoke to him yesterday and he snapped at me. He apologised afterwards and was all sweetness and light, so even great men can have hangovers, I suppose.' She pushed the folder across the desk. 'At least you and Captain Oliver will be old friends.'

'I'll walk as far as the beach before I go home,' said Kitty. 'It's going to be a fine evening and I love the sea at this time of the year. I take it that I arrange my off-duty to fit in with the rest of the staff. I'll be here early tomorrow to start duty.'

She walked out into the late afternoon sunshine, listening to the sounds of early spring—the birds singing and the trees in the avenue whispering. Daffodils blazed gold beneath the trees and although the trees were either winter green or bare, the softness of promised leaf burst was everywhere. She breathed deeply. This was one good reason for coming back home. Southampton and Birmingham had much to offer by way of company and entertainment, a faster speed of living and more intense work, but this was a part of her heritage, this island with its peaceful lanes and beaches and small vital towns that lived a bright existence once the false tinsel of tourism had been put away for the autumn, winter and early spring.

The winding driveway led her to the overgrown pathways to the beach. She saw again the remnants of the boathouse and the jetty. The dinghy belonging to the convalescent home was beached, as if someone had been inspecting it or even taking it out for an early sail. It might be fun to take some of the walking cases out for a break, and could be a valuable aid to rehabilitation, she thought. She walked down to the edge of the water and picked up a handful of dry sand. It was cold and as she looked at the sea, daylight fled and the deception that this was early summer was broken.

Turning, she moved back towards the main drive and the car park to collect her transport. A man in a wheelchair was making slow progress towards the Household Block. She quickened her pace. Whoever it was had a hard job as the path inclined up to the next bend and the gravel was very loose in many places. Whoever he was, he looked young and fit enough to make his own way, but as she caught up with him, he stopped as he heard her light footsteps.

'Ah, help at last,' he said and smiled sweetly.

'I can help you up the slope,' said Kitty.

'Thanks a lot. I saw you go down, actually, and I waited,' he said, leaning back and letting her take all the weight of the chair and of his considerable bulk.

She put her hands on the bar and the chair moved slowly up the slope. It was very difficult to obtain any purchase on the shifting gravel when she was wearing high heels and a tight belt. She began to wish that she had avoided him. 'You would be Captain Mycroft?' she asked, puffing slightly.

'The very same. One of the last of the halt the lame and the blind.'

'And almost ready to go home?'

'I shall never be ready. Who are you? A visitor to someone more lucky than me?'

'No, I am Sister Martin and I came to check with the staff here before coming on duty tomorrow.' She injected a little formality into her voice.

He swung round in his chair with such ease that she wondered just how incapacitated he could be. He grasped her hand and she stopped the chair. 'Great!' he said. 'I heard you were coming back. Old Oliver sings your praises so much that I am convinced that you kissed him goodnight.'

'That was not included in my schedule, Captain,' she said, coldly, and then heard the voice. She looked up to the stone terrace towards which the chair was being propelled.

A man was sitting on the wide balustrade of the terrace, his face almost in line with one of the carved beasts that sat with sightless stone eyes watching the driveway for invaders. But his eyes were alive. His eyes were alight with a fire that came from no stone, no man-made image. He reminded her of a hawk with glossy dark plumage and flashing stormy eyes. The bright blue track suit added to this illusion. A raven with blue tints to his feathers, she thought, and smiled. It was a ridiculous fantasy.

His eyes fixed an unsmiling gaze first on the man in the chair and then on her, and her smile died before the unwavering gaze. As she looked away, she knew that his eyes were a curious mixture of blue and grey, like a wild sea.

'What's happening to this place? You know what you should be doing right now, Captain?' he said grimly.

'I was tired and I wanted some fresh air.' The tone was sulky.

'You were due in Physiotherapy half an hour ago and the girl is waiting to leave for the day.'

'I was bored. This is the back of hell as far as I'm concerned and I saw Sister Martin and thought I'd say hello.'

'You are on the staff?' The words came like bullets of derision. 'Don't you ever look at notes to see what patients should be doing? Or do you think we want women in mufti pushing wheelchairs when there is work to be done?' He turned back to Captain Mycroft. 'I would be obliged if you would *walk* back to Physio and tell them that your session has been cancelled. Make an appointment for the morning and stick to it.'

Captain Mycroft swung out of the chair fairly easily and stood behind it, using it as a walker.

Sister Martin took a step to follow him. 'I can manage,' said the Captain. 'Better do as he says, Sister.' He lowered his voice. 'He's a right bastard. See you tomorrow morning.'

The man on the balustrade looked at her as if trying to place her. 'You said you were on the staff. I haven't seen you here.' His face was set in controlled anger and his fingers twisted an ivy leaf that had the nerve to grow near to his hand. 'If I ran this place permanently, it would be a crisper operation.'

She took a deep breath. If she was to work at the home, then this was the time to show the locum surgeon that she was not afraid of him, but she put out a hand to the cool stone to steady herself. 'I work for an agency and came in today only to check with the House Governor's office. I am not officially on duty until tomorrow morning. I worked here last year when some of the men came back from prolonged treatment after the Falklands. You were here, I believe, but I didn't nurse you, Commander.'

'You know me?'

'I know your name. I was told the names of staff when I went to the Governor's office. I was also told the names of the patients I shall deal with during this period of duty.'

'You haven't met Mycroft before today?'

'No, I met him in the drive down by the lane to the beach.'

'Didn't waste much time,' he said, and she couldn't know if he was referring to her or to the Captain.

'You know Oliver?'

She nodded. He mentioned one or two names and she nodded again. His lip curled and she was uncomfortable under the steely gaze.

'And they told you that the man with the hellish temper was Surgeon Commander Alexander Carlton Roscoe RN.' He spat out the words as if he gained a bitter satisfaction from hearing them.

'I was informed that you were now acting as locum for the resident doctor,' she said. 'I recall seeing you once when I was here.'

Her quiet dignity seemed to get through to him. 'I'm sorry,' he said, stiffly. 'Mycroft made me angry. He has no consideration for staff or the comfort of other residents here. If he did as he was told he could be discharged in a month.'

'Discharged? From here or from the army?' Anxiety made her forget that this man was hateful and rude. If Captain Mycroft faced discharge from his life's career, no wonder he was an awkward cuss.

'He is due for an assessing board in two weeks time and he could pass it if he would see sense.' He shook his head. 'I'm keeping you, Sister Martin. We shall no doubt be in touch whether we want to be or not.' He inclined his head in a mocking bow but remained seated on the wall. He called after her. 'I would like to see Malcolm, the porter. Would you be good enough to send him out here.'

She nodded, unable to speak. The arrogant, unspeakable man! Why couldn't he step inside the building and find the porter? It was all very well to be in charge but some men just threw their weight about as if by divine right.

She remembered the folder that she had taken to read in the office and knew it should be returned to the file. She walked into the long cool corridor and wished that she was wearing soft shoes. Her high heels tapped on the hard tiled floor and echoed even when she tried to walk on tip-toe. She reached the office after telling Malcolm that the Commander wanted to see him on the terrace and was surprised to see that the man smiled and didn't seem to resent being told what to do. She took a brief look once more at the files, and found those with Commander Roscoe on the cover. She refreshed her memory. He had been spattered with metal from mortar fire and had been operated on for their removal. And now, he was working in a minor post to finish his recovery.

As a nurse, she knew the value of the remedial room and swimming pool for cases that needed rehabilitation of muscles after such procedures, easing stiffness and making muscles strong again after inaction. But if he had suffered as the other men at the convalescent home had suffered, surely he must have sympathy with men like Captain Mycroft? She wondered when the terrifying man would be back at sea, unleashing his Captain Bligh temper on his unfortunate crew.

She walked back along the corridor and saw a wheelchair standing by a door. By force of habit, she pushed it along to the storage bay, knowing the rule about leaving chairs unattended outside rooms. The patients often used them to get back to the rooms and then forgot to ring to have them removed from the corridor. She turned the corner and the chair ran full tilt into the man standing by the window. He seized the arms of the chair to save himself and Kitty slid round on the high heels as if they pursued each other on a silly carousel. He leaned back against the wall and breathed deeply, and she was unable to stop until she came into sharp contact with his broad shoulder.

For a moment, she was acutely aware of his face touching hers. So the hard expression was only skin deep! His skin was firm and yet soft with a fragrance that reminded her of crushed bay leaves and pine needles. The dark hair was thick and silken. Quickly, she recovered and he swung the chair away, coming to face her. He rubbed his left leg and the eyes were grey in the half light, but burned brightly with a fire that was half anger and half pain.

'I'm sorry,' she gasped. 'Did I hurt you? I couldn't know you were there behind the door.'

'What are you doing? I thought you had gone and that Osborne could sleep safely. And don't you know better than to wear silly shoes with heels that can be heard from here to Cowes?' The grey eyes held a touch of blue. He reached out and absent-mindedly put a strand of her hair back where it belonged. She blushed furiously. 'Get out, will you? And change those stupid shoes before you come back.' He watched her go, the firm lips twitching as he saw her efforts to walk silently.

She could think of no reason for her unsteady walk. It must be anger that made her shake, she thought. He was such a prickly individual. Such lazy arrogance. She walked across the drive to the car park and put on her crash helmet. She had said she would work here again and she liked the place. Why should a man like him ruin her pleasure? She kick-started the engine and the moped started forward. It stalled and she had to do it again.

A face appeared in the unlit window of the Household dining room and watched her go, then the lights went on as a maid drew the curtains before dinner. Kitty put on her moped lights and joined the evening traffic. The road emptied as she came to the road from the junction turning to Wootton Creek. The lights across the river were soft and golden and would have brought a smile of contentment to her eyes on any other evening. He had had the gall to touch her, as if brushing back the hair a child had let hang over one eye. And his touch had been gentle, belying the threat of those relentless eyes. She shivered. Men like that were heroes and they must be strong to be effective in their chosen careers. They had to be hard to take what they had to face in war as he had had to face the enemy in the Southern Ocean.

She wanted to see him laugh, but knew that the sombre doctor in charge of the home would never smile at her with warmth. Any smile she attracted would be dry and derisive, as if she were a stupid female who had once annoyed him and hadn't the sense to keep out of his hair.

She wheeled the moped up the gangplank on the houseboat and leaned it under a shelf covered with a plastic sheet. The water gurgled under the keel as the tide went out and sea birds made a sleepy last journey to roost. Soon, the moon would climb over the bridge and light up the mudbanks left by the tide. She must trim the oil lamps that seemed the right kind of illumination on the old boat and which she used in preference to the connected electricity available. So, at a time when she was usually at peace with the world, why did she drop a mug and break it, and why did she find the cleaning of smoky glass tedious and decide that, for once, evening solitude was not for her?

'Damn,' she said as she opened the door to the fridge. No way could she get up enthusiasm for some wilted lettuce and dry cheese. Tomorrow, she must remember to buy in some stores. She packed

everything she might need for the following day
and zipped up the rucksack that held it all. The
evening stretched ahead with nothing to do but
read and watch TV or listen to tapes. Why wasn't it
enough?

On impulse, Kitty pulled on a warm anorak and
scarf and hoped she would be warm enough on the
way home. Her blue sweat shirt and cords were fine
but she found gloves and changed her shoes for
trainers. A large torch would light her back up the
gangplank on her return, and she smiled as she
looked forward to the cosy bar of the Sloop, one of
the pubs on the bridge. She walked through the
roughly levelled spinney bordering the water and
came to the road. Boats tilted at all kinds of odd
angles on the mud left by the departing tide, seeming as if they might disappear into the soft mudbanks, but she knew that, as the tide rose, the boats
would be refloated and ride the calm waters of the
Creek again.

When the tide turned, the burgees would sing
from the network of masts. She loved the sound.
She stopped before she came to the door of the
Sloop. Commander Roscoe had said her name. He
had called her Sister Martin. She frowned, trying to
recall if Captain Mycroft had used it, but she
couldn't remember. The memory of his eyes and
the touch of those solid shoulders stayed with her.
It was annoying that one man could ruin a perfectly
good evening. She escaped into the warmth and
smoke of the pub and felt strangely safe.

'Hi, Kitty!'

She waved and forced a path through the crowd at the bar and was met half way by a man in a shabby green army-surplus jacket and jeans.

'Paul! I thought you were in Salisbury.'

'Back today. Surprise all round. I thought you were working on the mainland, too.'

'Finished the job and guess where I am now?'

'At the local hospital? Or have you succumbed to psychiatric nursing at last?' He grinned. 'In that case, I could qualify for your full-time attention.'

'Not you. You are the most even-keeled man I know. Quite a change.'

'Meaning that someone isn't?' He handed her a half of bitter without asking what she wanted to drink. 'Here,' he said.

'How did you guess?' She laughed wryly. It was cosy talking to Paul Barton again, but slightly un-nerving. He seemed to read her thoughts and they managed to pick up conversations where they ended some time back, perhaps weeks ago. 'I'm back at Osborne for a while. It isn't the same. They have several of their usual bods there with relatives in tow. And some men from the Falklands who are back after yet more operations and treatment, but the staff have changes to let the regulars take leave.'

'And that is bad?'

'Not really.' She frowned. 'It shouldn't upset my routine there—I do know the place and most of the men I have to deal with while they are there. In a way, there will be too many, doing damn all. Most of the residents are ambulant and awaiting further assessment boards and the busiest department is Remedial and Physio.'

'But someone upset you.' His shrewd glance took in the frown and the sudden blush. 'Come on. Someone made a pass that offended you and you have to see him tomorrow.'

'Something like that.' She looked away. 'There's a new one there who might be difficult. He's an army captain. No, I think he's a marine. He pushed it a bit and I had to be firm.'

Why am I lying, and pretending that Mycroft upset me? she wondered. She could deal with him any day in ten minutes flat. Her air of graceful fragility had deceived many men into thinking that this was a sign of weakness and that she might be vulnerable to the more forceful charms of the average male chauvinist. She smiled, slightly.

'That's better. When you came in here tonight, you had a touch of the black dogs. You smile at everyone, remember? Tell Uncle Paul all your troubles and relax.'

'Oh, get lost! You should be on Ryde pier doing a mind-reading act.'

She tried to laugh naturally, but even in the warm bar with the approving gaze of Paul Barton boosting her ego and the thought of a good meal that she would have prepared for her in pleasant surroundings, she couldn't erase from her mind the steely eyes and that set jaw, the wide shoulders and the faint lines round a potentially generous mouth. He had been wounded and knew all about pain, so why was he so hard on Captain Mycroft? Pain brought tolerance to others once the personal damage was healed, or it should do. Experience led to understanding, they said, and besides being a wounded war hero, he was first of all a doctor, a healer and not some kind of . . . *Oberführer.*

Paul waved to another couple who joined them and after an hour of desultory conversation, Paul and Kitty went into the restaurant to eat. Paul insisted on buying the meal, while Kitty argued that if he did, then she must buy the wine. They sat by a window looking out on the moonlit sliver of water between the sand and mud. The ghost-like dinghies lay like stranded dabs. She glanced at Paul who was concentrating on taking the back-bone from a Dover sole. Quite the nicest man I know, she thought, and wondered why it did nothing for her libido. She bent over her fish and hoped that Paul wouldn't ask any more questions about Osborne.

How silly! She ought to be able to talk about Commander Roscoe and to laugh at his brusque and heartless manner, but she couldn't bring his name into the conversation. Just to think of him raised her blood pressure, or was it that her heart beat faster and made her pulse race? Her old sister tutor had been specific on that point. Pulse rate went up under temporary stress and if a girl was in love! It was an old joke that came out with moths flying out of it with every new influx of nurses. She felt her cheeks glowing. How stupid to think of that when she was smarting under the sting of one repulsive man. Commander Roscoe did nothing for her pulse rate, blood pressure or . . . libido. How could he after a ten minute encounter when he was very rude to her, and a sudden clash when he made it plain that she was a clumsy woman who couldn't keep her hair tidy? She put up a hand to brush the lock of hair away, recalling his hand on it, but it was neatly tied back and her hand fell away slowly to pick up her dessert spoon.

'How is your project going?' She forced her attention back to Paul, and then was safe in her own thoughts again as he told her in detail and for the next half an hour about the outline of the new book. He dwelt lovingly on certain discoveries he had made about families still bearing the same names as staff at Carisbrooke Castle when Charles I was imprisoned there before his execution. 'Fascinating,' she murmured at intervals, safe in the conviction that she would have found it so if she had been listening. But, with insistent regularity, her mind went back to the tall square-towered building by the sea. She resolved to add sailing shoes to her pack in case she could use the dinghy. Even if it was in her own time, it might be pleasant to relieve the boredom of the residents if they wanted to sail. It could be a valuable aid to recovery and the strengthening of unused muscles.

'Come on Saturday,' Paul said.

'Come where?'

'I *thought* you were far away. Not to worry. I like talking into a void. It sparks off ideas and you never interrupt me.' He smiled, indulgently. 'You take life too seriously. Why not be like me, Kitty. Relax.' He leaned forward. 'We get on fine, don't we?' She nodded. 'When can I move in with you?' Her eyebrows shot up. 'Come on, now, Kit. You've lived in that houseboat and wouldn't want to move, and I rather like it too. We could halve the rent and food bills. It would cost less for two than for two singles.'

'I have one sitting-room and one bedroom and some storage.'

'Grow up and join the big outside world, Kit. It would be cosy. In Pepys' day, whole families lived in one room, and in wayside inns, complete strangers slept in the same room, regardless of sex.'

'But not in the same bed. Mine is one double, not two singles.'

'As I said, cosy.'

She shook her head and he sighed. He didn't seem annoyed but she had a sneaking suspicion that he thought it only a matter of time before he moved in with her. Paul was outwardly placid and very good humoured, but there had been times when a hidden determination had surfaced for a moment, giving a slightly less favourable view of the man she sincerely liked. It showed now as he looked at his watch.

'Meeting someone?' she asked.

'A bloke on the local paper said he'd be here. I offered to buy him a drink. Excuse me while I look in the bar. I left a message that I'd be here, but he might have got caught up with some of the others out there.'

'Cheap publicity?'

Paul grinned. 'Why do my own barking? He wants stories and I can fill his column as often as he likes with facts that will appear in my forthcoming book.' He looked in the bar, then came back and shook his head. 'Not there yet. I told him that I had found some rather nice early editions in the library that I'm cataloguing. They'll give a boost to my next article if he gives me a mention next week. Remember, I am basically a historian and he writes local interest pieces.'

'What after this? I thought you had a job sorting out books and diaries in that manor they sold in West Wight?'

'That's next week. I can stay there while I do the work and wait for the sale of contents. I suggested they pay me enough to act as caretaker while I'm going through the papers and books.' He smiled. 'They were delighted and really quite grateful. They think I'm doing them a favour, but in fact, the cottage I'm in now has to go on the agent's books as a summer letting. He wants it by Easter. It was cheap for the winter but I can't afford seasonal prices.'

'So that's why you want to move in with me?' She tried to sound outraged but was forced to smile at his sheer nerve. 'No undying love involved? No vows of fidelity?'

'For ever, my darling Kitty, if you'll have me.' He seized her hand and kissed it, but she drew away. A week ago, she just might have fallen for it, convincing herself that he was good fun and something more.

'For ever? Or until the summer visitors go away and you can have a cheap cottage again?'

'For ever.' He was serious. 'At first, it was like that, but I find I want you rather badly, Kit. Don't keep me waiting. Please?'

'It wouldn't work. I know that for certain, Paul.'

'The trouble is that you need to see more of me. I'll come and meet you off duty tomorrow.'

'No, not at Osborne.' It was too quickly said and his eyes narrowed. 'I mean, not tomorrow. I'm not sure of my off duty and I shall have to play it by ear until I see where I'm needed. There are more staff than they told me at the agency but we need plenty of one-to-one treatment to keep the residents happy.'

'Working all hours? Not necessary. There are other nursing sisters there and you said yourself that the last time you were there all you had to do was to wheel men about in chairs. I know that they have to be able to do quite a lot for themselves or they wouldn't be acceptable in the home. Intelligent people can entertain themselves. They have each other and some have relatives handy, don't they?'

'It isn't quite like that.'

'Of course it is. You don't want to be used, do you? They have a perfectly good Physio unit and some occupational therapy. A little relaxing basket-making works wonders, so I'm told.'

'That's fine, after operations especially, but normally healthy soldiers and sailors are not the type for raffia work.' She smiled, suddenly picturing Commander Roscoe making a raffia mat. He had been a patient once and must have gone through the usual routine. He would swear rather forcefully if he had to wrestle with a recalcitrant basket. Paul noticed the tender half-smile.

'You shouldn't get involved. They come to Osborne and they go back to their wives.'

She started. Once more, Paul had put an unerring finger on the fact that she had not even considered. He would, of course, be married. Why hadn't she thought of that simple and blatantly obvious fact? Commander Roscoe was very handsome, if one liked eagles, was intelligent and a skilled surgeon, and one touch of his hair on her cheek with his face close to hers was enough to tell her that quite definitely he was very masculine and that his sexuality was burning like a sultry fire banked up under the constrictions of service life and the wounds he had suffered in the Southern Ocean. What did his wife think of him now, after he had suffered mortar fire in that brief sad war? Had it strained their relationship? Or was she even now living in the block reserved for the resident doctor, and would be seen walking the corridors of the lovely old house? He was back to normal and must want his wife with him.

To her relief, Paul saw the reporter hovering in the doorway. 'Be nice, there's a love. I want him to take my article to his editor and use these facts.' He put a folder on the table as if it had been there all evening and he just happened to have it with him. Paul was emerging as a much more calculating creature. Strange to feel this way when there had been other evenings when she had admired and envied his casual approach to life, his aptitude for getting by with the least possible effort and his general charm and humour.

Now, she watched him talking to the man, changing into a man's man who liked a slightly salty turn of humour, eyeing the passing women as if leching after them. This is going to end as a backslapping, drinks with the boys evening she thought, and murmured that she was going to the powder room. Paul nodded and went on with what he was saying.

She looked back from the door and saw the two heads together. The reporter was laughing and getting into just the right mood for Paul. There were more drinks on the table and Paul didn't even look up when she went back to pick up her bag. She went out into the cold air and took a deep breath. The moon was slim and pale and the sky clear as the tide whispered at the edges of the Creek, pushing back the flotsam on to the mud and teasing the boats erect at the moorings.

The houseboat moved as she went on board and she locked the hatch on her way down below. It had been a pleasant evening and had filled in the time well. She looked out of the porthole by her bed and loved the lift of the tide under her. A good evening. Paul was a good friend, if he could remain just that, with no favours on either side. He had amused her and her thoughts were a mixture of affection and irritation. That shirt he wore was more than a little grubby and his jeans were peppered with oil from his old boat which he anchored in the Creek. The soft lamplight was soothing and she loved the patina of the table left to her by her grandmother. The curtains were well laundered and the covers fresh. It was a very pretty boat, and comfortable.

Paul wouldn't fit in at all. She had a vision of Paul with dirty socks, and she was faintly revolted. She turned in bed and put out the light. What was wrong with her? All men had dirty socks. Even the august Commander. She giggled. It was rather like wondering if royalty ever went to the loo, as she had wondered when they visited the Island during her school days.

The Commander would think Paul a scruffy civilian, just a scruffy civilian.

CHAPTER TWO

'IT WOULD give your leg a rest,' said Sister Kitty Martin. 'This is what is so useful. At home, you might think you weren't dressed without the prosthesis, but here you can go wtihout it and nobody thinks twice about it.'

'That makes sense, Sister. All right, if you can really spare the time, I'd like it.'

'I'll fetch a wheelchair and we'll go now while the sun shines. Can you stay here in your room and I'll find a thick sock to keep the end warm before you venture out?' She smiled and went quickly to the office to check the morning medicines with the auxiliary nurse, so that she would be free to take Captain Rory Oliver for a turn round the park. She smiled, feeling that this was a small victory. Captain Oliver was very self-conscious about his lost foot, or had been until today when he seemed to be able to keep off the subject for at least an hour at a time.

'You'll need something warm, Sister,' he said. 'That uniform must be freezing out of doors.'

She laughed. 'I have a very thick cloak and I confess that under this dress is a very thin but effective garment made of insulating material, "as used on Everest", or so the advertisements say.'

'I know all about that. We used it in the Southern Ocean.'

She bit her lip. It was difficult to mention anything that didn't bring some reminder of the war in the Falkland Islands.

'I'll take a stick in case I want to see something. I can manage with one leg and a stick better than on crutches.' A matter of pride again, she thought. Anyone could use a walking stick and it showed that he was an active man with the ability to get about easily.

'Fine. If you want to bring glasses, you can watch anything in the Solent that passes.' She laughed. 'I suppose you haven't the same interest as the sailors among us. Lt Commander Sinclair spends most of his time upstairs looking at the passing ships through a huge telescope and the others hardly get a chance to use it.'

'The first buds of spring are enough for me,' he said. 'Funny how much this place reminds me of home.'

'You come from Devon, don't you?' The chair wheels moved freely and the air was good with a light breeze stirring the daffodils. 'Are you by the sea?'

'We have a farmhouse by the coast and when I come out of the Service, I shall rusticate and grow potatoes.' He looked ahead and his mouth tightened. 'It will be the best thing for a man with one leg.'

'One foot and the ability to lead a full life. You

were about to leave the Service in a few months, so you must have had your future planned in advance.' She waited but he didn't answer. 'What does your wife think of this? Has she green fingers or what it takes to grow things?'

He relaxed. 'No good expecting sympathy from you, Sister.'

'Every sympathy but no pity, Captain. You are all in one piece except for a small chip missing and you know it. What happened? Did you go home and wallow in the care and sympathy of your family and friends until you decided that you liked it very much better than being told to get on with life?' He flushed slightly. 'I'm sorry, I had no right to say that, but we do notice that when people come here they act much more normally without their loving families hanging on every word.'

He grinned. 'And it's wonderful to be here for that reason. I was up to here with sentimentality. My wife was fine, and she has always been wonderful, but the others made me feel as if I was a poor cripple who would have to be fed and cossetted for ever. My wife made me come back here to get sorted out.' He laughed. 'She was in the WAAF and stands no nonsense.'

'I hear the Physio girl is very pleased with you.'

'She told you?' He was pleased.

'She also said that you ought to swim and take more exercise. Have you been in the pool today?'

'Not today.'

'Nor yesterday, I believe.'

'You weren't here yesterday! You came today and you already know more than I do!'

'I do my homework. This afternoon, I suggest that you swim and exercise under water. Physio want you to do it and you will feel much better if you see yourself doing something you were good at before the accident.'

'Will you come too?' He looked up, his pleasant craggy face oddly pleading. So he wasn't really ready for the big outside world.

'I'm off this afternoon,' she said. He looked disappointed. 'But I'd love a swim. I have my things with me. We'd better get back now as I see a large and black cloud over there.' She turned the chair to face the building, and when two residents and their wives passed them, Captain Oliver seemed quite unconcerned that he was in a chair with his leg in a bright blue bed sock showing clearly that he had no left foot.

'Time to go for therapy,' he said. 'I have to wear the thing for a few hours today and more tomorrow so that the shape of my stump is kept right for the fitting. I can't say I'm looking forward to it, but the sooner I can take it for granted, the sooner I can plan again.'

'You're doing very well, according to your notes. We shan't have the pleasure of your company for much longer.'

'I have to thank this place for many things, Sister. I couldn't think clearly until I came here the first time, and it was a goal to reach, to come back and complete the treatment. I wish my wife could be here but she has the house to run and is busily buying in hens, and I think a goat now that I am out of the way.'

'You see! By the time you are home again for good, you will be a true son of the soil.'

'Not really. I am better with mechanics and engines. Sister Bowen was telling me that her husband is a marine engineer at Cowes. That really would interest me.' He was silent until they climbed the slope to the terrace. 'I have a large boat shed in bad repair. I might be able to do something there.' He bent suddenly to touch his injured leg. 'Hell! It's happening again.'

'Is it painful?'

'No, just itching.' He gave a forced laugh. 'Maybe I'm growing another foot.'

'Some people have more trouble with a phantom foot than others. Let me hold your leg and rub your calf muscles.' She turned the chair so that it couldn't run away and put on the brake. He held her shoulder to keep himself from falling from the chair as the absent foot continued to itch. Firmly, she stroked the leg until the spasm passed. He bent to kiss her cheek and she smiled.

'You're great,' he said in a gruff voice. 'No fuss and you make me feel a man again.'

'My pleasure.' She stood up and laughed. 'But the Physio girl will wonder where you are. Come on, we'd better hurry.' She wheeled him into the building and saw the Commander leaning non-

chalantly against a pillar, staring into space. He
looked cross and didn't seem to see them, although
he must have seen them coming along the terrace.
It was only when she had left Captain Oliver in the
physical education room that she remembered the
innocent and spontaneous kiss that the Captain had
pressed on her cheek. From the house, it might
have looked as if she was embracing the man in the
wheelchair.

She consulted her list of duties and found to her
dismay that Bruce Mycroft had sprained an ankle
while fooling about on the exercise bars and needed
pushing round the grounds for half an hour to get
fresh air. She wondered who had ordered that
treatment and if it was Mycroft's own suggestion.
He was quite capable of propelling himself along in
the self-manipulated chairs.

'Nurse?' she said as she came to her office. 'Are
you free for half an hour?' But it was time for the
auxiliary nurse to go to lunch as she had been
instructed at morning report. There was no escape.
She glanced at the duty list and saw that Bruce
Mycroft's name had been added in a hurry by
someone whose writing she didn't recognise.
Perhaps the Commander had written it, as he was
in charge. She shrugged and pulled her belt tight as
if bracing herself to meet an enemy. The uniform
dress was crisp and spotless and well cut, showing
the good lines of her figure. Usually, her appearance on duty gave her confidence and she took a
great pride in being immaculate. She glanced down

at the white shoes with medium heels and noiseless tread and rubbed them with tissue to remove traces of dust from the gravel paths. Twice, she adjusted her hair, although it lay in a glossy roll away from her collar and the small cap perched on it looked at once crisp and pert. I'm getting neurotic about my appearance, she thought. I know I look smart, so what does it matter if one sarcastic man thinks I'm a fool?

She walked slowly to the front entrance for a chair. I wonder if he does any work, she thought, resentfully. Each time she had seen him so far, he was lounging with that arrogant lord-of-all-I-survey expression, and he had been too lazy to go in search of the porter. And for a doctor in charge to wear a track suit, even if it was very masculine and well kept, seemed a little too individualistic for a place that served the officers of Her Majesty's Services. He was a conceited prig who thought that his record was enough to give him privileges above his posting.

Almost to her relief, he had gone and she took the chair along to Captain Mycroft. He greeted her with a grin. 'Are you ready?' she said, and held the chair ready.

Mycroft walked with hardly a limp across the floor. He stood by the chair and looked down at her. 'The luck of the draw,' he said and laughed. 'And I get the prize. I was praying that it wouldn't be the fat one with the bottle-shaped legs.' He eyed her with insolent appraisal. 'Very smart, very crisp and, as our splendid Commander would no doubt say, I love the cut of your jib.'

'I am quite sure he would say no such thing,' she said. It was impossible to take offence but she knew that she needed to be careful with this man. He was typical of a healthy man with time and energy on his hands, who was not even greatly incapacitated. Brought up in New Zealand, he had come to the UK to university and taken his commission from there. She knew she had to make allowances for a certain brashness and forwardness that was a feature of most men she had met from down-under.

'I doubt if you need this chair. Let me see you walk across the floor,' she said.

'Just for you, Sister.' He walked with an exaggerated limp and screwed up his face as if in pain.

'Sister Martin?' She turned sharply towards the voice and saw the Commander standing in the doorway, his face set and his eyes cold. Her heart sank. Not again! Was it something she'd done?

'Yes, Commander Roscoe?'

'What are you doing in this room?'

'I was about to take Captain Mycroft out on the terrace in a chair.'

'Why?' The voice was low and deceptively silken.

'His name was on the duty list and I was available before lunch. The juniors have gone to first sitting.' The Commander looked from her to Mycroft and back. 'I was doing my duty,' she said, unable to bear the silence. She looked at Captain Mycroft and saw that he was red-faced and uncomfortable. 'What is it?' she said. 'Your name was on the list and I had heard about your ankle.'

The grey eyes softened slightly. 'What ankle, what list, Captain?' He spoke to Mycroft but his gaze was on the slim and pretty sister who looked cross and embarrassed.

'All right, so I wrote my name in the book and told the night nurse that I had sprained my ankle and couldn't get up for a bath this morning.'

'So she had to bath you, or at least wait on you in bed?'

'No harm done. She didn't mind.'

'And you waste a nursing sister's valuable time and energy making her do a job that any rating could do.' The grey eyes were unfaltering and the Captain shuffled and tried to laugh. 'Sister, I have work for you that can't wait.' It was as if the Captain didn't exist. 'Please collect your cloak and whatever you need to take with you. One of my subs needs a scan and the ambulance leaves in five minutes.'

'Ryde hospital?'

He nodded and she left the room, hurrying back to her office and leaving a note for the nurse coming back from lunch. She went to the car park and saw the ambulance backed up to the entrance. She hurried and the driver waved a hand in greeting. 'Is he in there?' He nodded and she went to the back of the vehicle thinking that she should travel with the patient. She gasped. There were two men in the back. One she recognised as the man needing the scan and the other long body, reclining lazily on one elbow, was the Commander. She wondered how long he would take to finish talking to the patient and to leave, but he grinned slightly.

'I'm going too. You'll have to ride shotgun with the driver, Sister.' The use of the American phrase was relaxed and amused.

'Do you really need me to come?' She looked at the man on the other bed. He looked healthy enough and if the Commander was accompanying him, no nurse was necessary, and, as a minor detail, she was hungry. The first sitting for lunch would now be over and Kitty was aware that she had eaten nothing but one slice of toast for breakfast. This sinking feeling must be due to lack of food and not to the dread of facing the man who now eyed her with cool appraisal, stretched out like a sinuous cat, taking all the length of the bed with his tall frame. He still wore a smart blue track suit and he looked like a taut-muscled athlete taking his ease before embarking on a marathon run or something equally strenuous.

'Of course I need you,' he said. 'The rule is that no resident travels without a nurse in an ambulance.' It was smoothly said and convincing, if the person to whom he was talking didn't know that it was a lie. She bit her lip but refrained from the retort that sprang to her mind. The brute. He wanted her to miss lunch and to be forced away from Captain Mycroft. She had met people in her own profession who pulled rank to get their own petty ends, and he must be one of these. And yet the staff at the home liked him and respected his judgment . . .

'Very well,' she said. 'Have you any idea how long this visit will take?'

'Does it matter?' The thick eyebrows were level and the eyes grey-dark.

'Not really, but I should be allowed time for lunch, unless that is now a new rule, too.'

He smiled, slowly, and she blushed, knowing that he knew she had seen through his excuse for getting her away from the gallant captain. 'We could put you on a drip feed,' he said, 'if it is so urgent.'

'No, I can get something at the nurses' cafeteria if you let me know when to report back to the ambulance.'

'Give us an hour and check with Reception,' he said, briskly, and she knew that he expected her to join the driver.

'All the officers crocking up again?' said the driver. 'We haven't done much with your lot for some time, Sister. Remember you from a year or so back when we had the first lot back from the Argies.' He chatted on and the words droned over her head, requiring only a nod and a surprised, 'Really' from time to time. 'Going to X-ray, aren't they?'

'The Sub-Lieutenant is going there,' she said.

'The Commander usually goes for his checks by car. Is he okay, Sister?'

'Fine as far as I know. I thought he was fully recovered and just doing this locum as a feedback into service life full time.'

'Could be.' The man shrugged and turned into the drive of the hospital that had served the Island well for so many years, expanding and improving so much that there was less and less need to use the mainland hospitals for treatment of any but the most complicated cases.

Kitty climbed down from the cab and went to the back door. She handed the Lieutenant two sticks and he leaned heavily to one side as he walked slowly to the entrance. Commander Roscoe was looking at some notes and sat on the rear end of the ambulance with his feet on the ground. He glanced up. 'Take him to X-ray, Sister. I'll be in to see Harrison in five minutes, if you would be good enough to give that message to Reception.'

The girl at the desk smiled. 'Nice to see you again, Sister.' She jotted down the message and reached for the phone to bleep Mr Harrison, the senior surgeon on duty. 'How is that wonderful man?' she laughed. 'Everyone gets a fast pulse on the days he comes here. Lucky people who nursed him.'

'I didn't have that pleasure,' said Kitty. How could she say that the man that women drooled over was a hard, sarcastic bore who seemed to single her out for the sharp edge of his tongue?

'Does he come here often?'

The girl laughed. 'Sounds as if he dances! Well, he might one day. But here? I've seen him three times in the past week and Mr Harrison and he are old buddies.'

So he skives off to visit old buddies instead of making sure his department runs smoothly, thought Kitty. He looks so lazy and self-satisfied when he isn't looking like thunder . . . at me.

'I'll be in the cafeteria, if I'm needed,' she said. 'I shall be back here in an hour and I can be ready before then if they want me.' She walked quickly away to find something to eat before the Commander sent for her on another feeble excuse. Lunch time was nearly over and she took a salad and two wholemeal rolls with butter and cheese as the hot dishes were past their best. She ate alone and tried to think of anything but the man who forced his personality into her every conscious and unconscious thought. Damn him, she told herself. I'll ask Paul if he still wants to shack up with me. That should take my mind off stone griffins. The memory of his profile against the pale sky, lined up with the stone beasts protecting the terrace of Osborne had stayed with her, as if he was a part of the old building and its history of royal service.

The Queen's beasts, they said in heraldry. He was like that, strong and implacable against the Queen's enemies and against any who displeased him. And I am enemy Number One for some obscure reason, she thought, and was sad. He was a perfect specimen of masculine health, with a wonderful face and the kind of mouth that would hush a woman's protests if he wanted her enough. She stared at the blank wall and decided to take a walk. To think of him as a male chauvinist was one thing, but to let her imagination dwell on the more intimate aspects of his life and sexual potential was stupid and dangerous.

It was chilly outside, dressed in uniform, even with her thick cloak tightly round her, so she went back to Reception to get warm and to wait for the returning men. The ambulance driver came back to the desk. He had been eating a snack with some of the porters and he was hurrying, as if he was late.

'Are we going?' Kitty asked.

'I'm taking the young officer back, Sister. He's had his X-rays, and Mr Roscoe is staying.'

'I'll be with you in two minutes.'

'Not you, Sister. The Commander wants you to wait for him. He'll be coming back by car. He left it here the day before yesterday when he saw Mr Harrison and had a lift in the ambulance back to Osborne.'

'But I came with the patient.'

'That's what my orders are, Sister.' The man picked up his work sheet and a red blanket that belonged in the ambulance and pushed on the swing doors. Kitty stared after him. The man must be mad. One minute he said that it was a rule for a nurse to go with a patient in the ambulance and now

he was calmly sending the ambulance back unattended and was going back by car.

She paced the floor until she found that she was
attracting attention so she sat on the hard bench
where hundreds of waiting patients had sat over the
years. Time was passing slowly but inexorably. It
was mid-afternoon and she had to hand over to the
next sister on duty before she went off duty. It was a
good thing that the department was slack and that
no one needed skilled attention, but to be away,
kicking her heels, and then go off duty was not very
good. Where was the man? She fumed in silence.
Was this all part of his 'hate Sister Martin'
campaign?

The doors of the lift opened at the end of the
corridor and Mr Harrison strode towards her.
'Hello, Sister Martin. When are you coming back
to us here?' His rather ugly face was full of friendly
warmth. 'Don't let that so-and-so work you to
death, Sister. He wanted to get you into the theatre
this afternoon. He helped me out by assisting with a
perforated appendix and wanted you to hold a
retractor when I heard that you were here and told
him how good you are in theatre.'

'I'm sorry. I was having lunch. I didn't get a
message, or I would have come, Mr Harrison.'

'He changed his mind.' He laughed. 'Said you
saw enough of him at Osborne and wouldn't want
to see him in action here.' He felt in his pocket.
'Damn. I had this for him.' It was a sealed envelope. He produced a second one identical with

the first but with the Sub-Lieutenant's name on it.
One for the Commander and one for the other
man? They were the kind of envelopes in which
reports were sent. 'Just the results of the X-rays. I
left the wet plates in the surgeons' room and the
radiographer assessed them so that Roscoe could
take them back with him. Could you pop up to
theatre and say that they are complete in case he
waits around for them?' He smiled. 'Good to see
him working again, and good for him to do something other than sitting on his ass. He should be
finished. I left him to close up. Must go. I have to
see two PPs before five o'clock.'

Kitty smiled to herself. So he had had to do some
work for a change. Mr Harrison had made him help
and then pleaded his appointments as an excuse to
leave him to finish. Well, well, did Mr Harrison
think he had become lazy, too?

The lift took her swiftly to the theatre floor and
she walked the familiar corridor to the surgeons'
room which could be reached from the outer corridor. Lights shone in the sterilising room and in the
main theatre the central beam was off. She saw
figures in the theatre and thought that he must be
there, and that it was safe to go into the surgeons'
room. She *did* tap on the door, or so she thought,
but whoever was in there didn't hear until she
pushed the door open and stood transfixed at what
she saw.

The door leading to the theatre from the room
was firmly closed and the door to the shower room

was half open. Too late, Sister Kitty Martin recalled that only operating staff used the outer door while operations were in progress. This was to prevent anyone from walking into the theatre from the outside corridor wearing clothes worn outside the hospital. The nursing staff had their own duty and changing rooms on the other side, where the same rule applied. Messages were handed in through the central anaesthetic room by nurses in uniform. She was a nurse in uniform and should have gone to the middle door!

A man was drying himself with a large hospital towel. His skin was still wet across his back, and as the towel moved, the broad and muscular back was exposed and the taut buttocks tensed with effort as he tried to reach the fallen towel. Kitty stared, not at the beautiful nudity of the man as this was nothing new to any nurse of her experience, but at the scars that puckered one side of his back. He struggled to reach the towel again but he found it difficult to bend sideways and the skin pulled against the healed lines of surgery.

If he had been a patient under her care, sent to bath and needing help, Kitty would have gone to him and even helped to dry the parts of his back that he couldn't reach, but this was Commander Roscoe, the man in charge of the convalescent home, who would resent her help. She backed away and stepped sideways to the other door, opening it softly and then going into the chaos of the post-operative anaesthetic room. 'Anyone at home?' she called in a clear voice. 'Mr Harrison sent me up with some papers for the Commander.'

A nurse came forward, hitching up her over-long gown. 'He's in there. Should be ready by now. I was just going to take the coffee into him. Mr Harrison couldn't wait.' She looked hot and cross. 'I hate emergencies. We're very short-staffed.'

'Give me the tray, Nurse. If you would make sure he's decent, I'll take it in with the letters.'

The nurse grinned. 'Worried in case you see more than you should? I wouldn't be. Even those scars are sexy.'

'You've seen them?' She didn't know why she was surprised. In this context, scars were commonplace and he had been a patient who got used to female staff seeing his bare limbs. Was it her own feeling she was considering and not his possible discomfiture? He would grin and possibly ask her to dry his back, wouldn't he? So why be shy after all her experience nursing male patients?

'I peeked,' said the nurse cheerfully. 'He wanted a tee-shirt to wear under his sterile gown and I barged in when Mr Harrison was examining his back. When he came into the theatre, he was covered. Silly man,' she said, tenderly. 'He's a hero and any wounds he got in the Falklands are badges of courage.'

'Mr Harrison was examining him?'

'Professional curiosity, I suppose. You don't mind taking the tray?' The nurse tapped on the door of the surgeons' room from the theatre end and a deep voice called come in. Kitty walked in with the tray, her eyes downcast as if concentrating on the task. He swept some clothes from the table and she set the tray down before him.

'Thank you, Sister. Why are you here?'

'Mr Harrison asked me to bring you these.' She handed him the envelopes, and made for the door.

'Stay,' he ordered. 'Pour me some coffee and take a cup yourself. I see there are two cups and Harrison couldn't wait.'

She hesitated, her shoulders tense, then shrugged and did as he said. He was wearing a brushed cotton shirt of the same royal blue as the track suit which lay across a chair. He wore theatre trousers which must have been put on in a hurry when the nurse tapped on the door, and his feet were bare. Thick socks lay ready to put on, folded back in the way that made them easy to don, a relic from the days when he couldn't bend sufficiently after his operation.

She sipped the good coffee and wondered why it tasted better when drunk in such surroundings. She had tasted coffee in many theatres and in cafés and restaurants, and she thought that it had a special flavour amid the wreckage of an operating theatre after a list.

He put the envelopes into his briefcase and she saw the tightening of his mouth before he reached for his cup. 'I hope I haven't kept you waiting,' he said, formally.

'I'm on duty, and you told me to come,' she said.

'I ought to telephone to hand over to the next sister in charge if you don't plan to go back yet.'

'That means you are off duty?'

'It isn't important,' she said, quickly. 'I intend going back to see that everything is all right. I often stay in my off duty if someone wants help in the pool.'

'And give out tea and sympathy? Loads of pity to make them feel good?'

'No! Not like that.' He was sneering at her again. 'Patients need to talk sometimes and it comes easily in a more relaxed and possibly social atmosphere.'

He stepped towards her and helped himself to more coffee, but put the cup back on the table. He seemed to tower above her and she realised with a sense of shock that she had never seen him at his full height except reclining in the ambulance. She found his nearness stifling and knew that she was breathing unevenly. The thin cotton trousers clung to him where he had failed to dry one leg and his thigh. She was reminded of a pirate in a blue shirt and white cotton pants. But he needed no cutlass to make him a man of power. His hands were on her shoulders and he looked down into her eyes with an expression that was both enquiring and puzzled. 'And do they tell you all?'

'I never ask, and what I am told I never divulge if it is in confidence,' she said, simply. 'It's all a part of the work. You must know that, Commander.'

He regarded her carefully, almost stripping her with that penetrating blue-grey stare. 'Nuns lead men to confession. Nuns and goddesses make mortals confess and seek absolution.' His smile was suddenly weary. 'And we have so much that we regret.'

'I am not a nun and I only listen. I would never want to hear anything that a man was reluctant to tell me.' Her colour rose and she could smell the faint aroma of the skin paint used in the theatre. It was clean and sharp and oddly erotic, like a shared memory of a man naked out of the shower.

'No,' he said, slowly. 'I can't imagine you a nun. That leaves a goddess.' He smiled with such sweetness that her mind clouded. His grip tightened. 'How far does your care take you? Like this?'

His mouth seemed to be on hers without him moving. His hands dug into her flesh as if he wanted to leave scars on the creamy skin under the crisp white dress. There was longing and the throb of hidden frustration in his touch and as his kiss became a release of passion, she forced her mouth away, shaking, and with her eyes shocked and filled with tears. She wanted to run away, to hide and never to see him again, but she was unable to do more than stand and look up at him through her tears.

He turned away. 'I'm sorry. That was unpardonable. It was just that you look so damned virginal in all that white and it can't be true.'

'Why not?' she whispered.

'I'm sorry,' he repeated. He was fast regaining control and his anger flared. 'Why the hell did you come to us? Isn't it bad enough to have men without wives and girl friends, without seeing women with figures to drive any sane man mad?'

'I don't do that.'

'Mycroft is out of hand and sets a bad example. Even Oliver who is safely and happily married isn't immune.'

'That's not fair. All he does is talk of his family and he is longing to get back to them.' She tried to smile to show that his outburst was forgiven. 'That's what they all want, to get back to normal, and we understand that. You are well again but you haven't picked up the threads of your career and all the other parts of living.' She couldn't bring herself to say that he needed to be with his wife or girl friend and that it was natural to be physically attracted to any woman with youth and a good body. She didn't know yet if he was married.

'Stop being so damned fair,' he stormed. 'Go and use the phone and meet me at the car in ten minutes.' He called her back. 'And Sister Martin. Fix that cap. It's a disgrace. You can't go downstairs looking as if . . . someone attacked you.'

She was left facing the door that he slammed shut. So that's how it was. He slammed a door on what he didn't want to see. She remembered the letters in his briefcase and wondered if he was putting off reading them, and needing the reassurance of physical contact to give him courage to do so. She hurried to the phone, dismissing her thoughts as stupid. He was just another man trying it on for size and wondering if she was promiscuous. Mycroft had much to answer for if he had given that impression.

She found the number and got through quickly. Everything had been boringly peaceful all the afternoon, with Captain Mycroft actually pushing another patient in a wheelchair and being very helpful.

'So you don't need me there? You're sure?' She put back the phone. Her moped was at the Home so she would have to appear briefly to collect it and her outdoor clothes. She walked down to the car park and saw the Commander sitting in the driver's seat of a large dark green car with luxurious hide upholstery and soft rust velvet cushions. She paused to recover her courage. The hawklike head seemed even more arrogant as the breeze caught his dark hair and made the grey eyes glint in the afternoon light.

'Do you have to go back now?' he asked. It was as if nothing had happened between them.

'I have to collect my transport,' she said. He waited until she had fixed her seat belt, then started the engine. His hands on the wheel rested gently with latent power and she could not equate them with the near violence of his grip on her shoulders. He was two men who showed separate faces and she was thoroughly confused. If he was attracted to her, why not say so and it might lead to something beautiful? But one glance at the autocractic profile told her that he had not reached that stage in his career without knowing all about women and love and there must be someone to whom he was bound by marriage, love or lust.

He drove over part of the same road that she would have to cover on her way home. She sighed and looked back, thinking it was a waste to be going to Osborne and then back as if going on the Ryde road again. He glanced down as she sighed, as if wanting an explanation. 'I live at Wootton,' she said, 'and I shall have to come this way again tonight.'

'In one of these houses?' They were passing a strip of ribbon development.

'No.' Her disgust seemed to amuse him. 'I have a houseboat on the Creek.'

He slowed the car and she saw him smile. 'You are full of surprises, Sister Martin. I didn't know you lived on the Island.'

'I have to live somewhere,' she said, ungraciously. She wouldn't tell him that this was the place she loved above all the places in which she had worked. It was none of his concern.

'That's good, to think you are local,' he said, smiling. She looked up, wondering if he could begin to care about her as a woman and not as a nursing sister or a play object, but she decided that he ran true to form. 'You can help us out in the theatre when you are working in any of the local hospitals.' He grinned. 'You were good enough to say you liked giving up your off duty for the halt and lame.'

'But you fit in to neither category, Commander,' she said.

They came to the high gates and swept along the curving gravel. He drew up at the entrance and she opened her door. 'I'll park the car, Sister. Go carefully, and I'll see you in your office tomorrow at ten.'

She glanced back as she went up the steps to get her out-door clothes and helmet and he was watching her go. He started the car and made a U-turn and was still there when she went into the building.

CHAPTER THREE

THE night sister looked at her watch. 'What kept you?'

'I'm very sorry. I had trouble with the bike and had to take the bus.' Kitty Martin held up a grimy hand. 'I didn't stop to clean up as I didn't want to make you late off. The garage will drop the bike here later.'

'It's all right, you aren't late.' Sister smiled. 'But seeing you come up the drive as if the devil was after you, I had to tease you a little.'

'Thanks,' said Kitty, drily. 'I'll scrub my hands and be with you in five minutes.' She quickly changed from her boots and jacket, stripping off the warm shirt and shivering slightly as the cold cotton dress slid over her shoulders. It was as if she lived two lives and could strip off one and put on the other at a moment's notice. The efficient nursing sister took over from the slightly rumpled and unskilled motor mechanic. She made a silent vow to sell the infernal machine and to buy a second-hand car. For a long time, the idea of going anywhere where her appearance mattered had nagged at her when she arrived carrying a white helmet under one arm, her face pink with fresh air and her hair untidy, and as she had walked up the long drive to Osborne, the tall elegant frontage had looked down on her with blank derision. And behind the windows, had there been other eyes besides those of the night sister, laughing at her progress? It was all so undignified.

'A quiet night with nothing much to report,' Sister said. 'Captain Mycroft slept well, much to the relief of all concerned, and he has yet to surface. The quiet one in Room Six seems to be in pain again and I want the Commander to see him—Basil Sinclair. You have met him, haven't you?'

'Yes, he was here the last time I came to nurse here. He had several pieces of shrapnel in his body and legs and they could only remove some of them. I remember that someone told me he was with the Commander when they were both wounded.'

'He has one piece left that they wanted to leave in the hope that it might move away from his spine. It's in a tricky position. Between you and me, I think the decision was his. He had so much surgery that he just couldn't face any more.'

'So he spends most of his time up in the observation tower looking at passing ships and hoping that nobody will notice him?'

'That's right. We sent him over to the naval hospital for assessment and with a private message that he should have further X-rays. They've come back and the metal hasn't moved away. In fact, it seems closer, but I want the Commander to see it. The new plates will come from the hospital by special carrier, possibly by helicopter.'

'That sounds serious.'

'Not necessarily, but you know the services. Everything at the double.'

'I hope they are here by ten. That's when we have a visitation.'

'You don't like our lovely Alex?'

'If you mean Commander Roscoe, then *no*! I was much happier when I was here the last time. We were busy and everyone cared. There was no time for people like Bruce Mycroft or men with an over-inflated sense of their own importance.'

'Didn't fall off that bike and hit your head, did you?'

'Sorry.' Kitty smiled. 'It was the bike. It made me bad-tempered, and I hate to see Mycroft goosing anything in skirts who comes within five yards of him. Basil is a very nice guy and deserves better.'

'Well, have coffee and cool it. Himself will be here at ten ack emma and we should be on the ball.'

As the minute hand swung round to ten, she tidied the papers on her desk for the third time. The rooms were quiet, the drug round was done and there were no dressings until later. In fact there was no way of escaping the Commander when he made his round. The telephone rang and her hand flew to it.

'I would like to speak to Commander Roscoe.' The voice was husky and assured. 'I'm Carol Gaynor.'

'May I take a message or a number that he can ring? He is due here in a few minutes.' She heard a sound at the door and looked up. 'Oh, here he is. How fortunate.' He leaned over the desk and took the receiver.

'Carol . . . darling.' There was a lilt in his voice that Kitty had never heard. 'Oh, this is splendid. It's very good to hear your voice.' He paused and Kitty could only wonder what the husky voice was saying. 'Of course. You must come as soon as you can make it.' His eyes held a tender light. 'My dear, we have a lot to discuss. I can't tell you how important this visit will be. You are staying at East Cowes? Good. That makes it so easy.' He let the receiver slip back on the rest as if it was made of some precious material, and when he looked at Kitty, his eyes were blue as if the sun was shining after a storm. His mouth still held the softness reserved for small creatures and for people much beloved. He looked down at his comfortable clothes. 'I shall have to change into something more appropriate,' he said.

A call came for Kitty to see the housekeeper about linen and she excused herself once he was reading the night report and the new notes and X-rays. She couldn't bear to stay with him and to be included in the aura of benevolence he had assumed after the telephone call. He frowned as he saw the X-rays which had come in a hurry in a fast car from the heliport, and Kitty saw that this did something to dim his pleasure a little. Surely all his rudeness couldn't be the fault of one husky-voiced woman who had his heart in thrall? Would he allow his private feelings to rule him so much that he was unpleasant to another woman to console himself for his own frustration?

She avoided him when she saw him walking slowly down past the rooms, with a nurse carrying the notes and X-rays on a well-oiled trolley, and when he sent a message asking her to come to the office, she was at lunch.

It was a relief to have the afternoon off. She was half way to the car park before she remembered that she had promised to take Captain Oliver to the hot bath because she had been held up the day before. She looked around, cautiously, to make sure that she was unobserved. This was quite ridiculous. What did it matter if he saw her? She was officially off duty until the evening and had every right to use the pool if she wanted to help a patient. She turned to go back and saw a long sleek sports car draw up at the visitors' entrance. The girl who stepped out was blonde and slim with long legs and the kind of body that makes men slaves. Her simple loose coat swung back over a matching suit of speedwell blue and every accessory matched with the precision that the Commander would view with complete approval. Kitty Martin was miserable as she went back to her office to collect her swimming things. The blonde would be the perfect wife for a man who loved order and beauty combined.

She went to the staff room to tell a nurse on duty that she would collect Captain Oliver in one hour for his swim, and, to kill time, she wandered round the outside of the State Apartments of the Royal house of Osborne, now closed until Easter when crowds of visitors would throng the carefully fenced-off grounds and the living rooms that she had been the home of Victoria's family. Although she had been through the rooms on many occasions, they still held an aura of a home and not a stately building with no soul. Here, the young queen had been able to get away from affairs of state, her children had run free in the sun and breezes and had even dug their own gardens with miniature tools. Kitty wondered if the pastry that they made in the Swiss cottage with its small kitchen and full range of equipment, had been as tough and grey as that made by less famous children.

She was grateful for the peace and serenity. The walk back to the Household Block came all too soon and her heart beat faster, wondering if the Commander and his girl friend would be safely out of the way. What is happening to me? she wondered with dread. Two days ago I was perfectly content with my life style, my job and even with Paul as a casual boy friend, but now, as soon as I see one abrasive man who doesn't like me one little bit, I shy away as if he might bite me. And yet I want to know what he is doing, who is with him and if he thinks of me. Resolutely, she collected the Captain and took him to the bath.

'I told the girl in Remedial and she said that she will be there with two of the others and will be glad of your help, if only to keep an eye on us while she is busy doing treatments,' he said. 'Are you sure that you want to give up your free time?'

'Sheer luxury,' she said, and almost believed that she was enjoying herself when she was immersed in the pleasantly warm water that did so much to relax stiff muscles and reluctant joints. Captain Oliver slid into the water. His wound had healed and was ready to stand swimming-bath water and his pleasure in being completely mobile, suspended in the warmth, was rewarding.

'I shall do this at home. There's a good pool in the local university and I know one of the professors there who will let me have the use of it, and when I return to duty, I can use the Army facilities as it's unlikely that I shall be posted to an active unit.'

Kitty Martin smiled. So he was already thinking about joining the fit and the able-bodied again. And when she saw him later, walking along the corridor with just a stick to give him confidence, she knew that the miracle of healing was almost complete.

'I'll take him to the gym now,' said the remedial therapist. 'Thanks for your help, Sister.'

'My pleasure,' she said, and waved to Captain Oliver as she went to change back into her civilian clothes. I am off duty for another two hours, she thought as she brushed her hair under the hot-air dryer. What could she do in that time? Wootton was too far away to visit in such a short time and she would be going home there after duty tonight. To stay in the building wasting the sunshine seemed stupid and she wasn't hungry enough to find a café and eat toasted buns and coffee as some of the others liked to do. The sunshine was too good to waste, but she wished that she knew where to go.

She pinned her hair into a French pleat to keep it from curling and becoming unmanageable when she had to put it under her cap once more, hoping that it was dry enough to put under her crash helmet while she drove her moped to the chain ferry. She zipped up the front of her dark blue padded jacket and pulled on the high-heeled boots that were both practical and goodlooking on the bike. Looking like a slim despatch rider, she walked to the car park, her body relaxed and glowing after the pool. The sports car was still there and she imagined the handsome couple laughing and making love in the Captain's room and he with that wonderful expression of tenderness in his blue-grey eyes. She sat astride the moped and kick-started, seeing the sports car out of the tail of her eye.

The lovely blonde woman was walking slowly towards the car, with Commander Roscoe beside her. She looked up into his face, anxiously, and Kitty saw him shake his head as if dismissing what she said.

She smiled gently and put a hand to his cheek. He held the hand and put it to his lips and even from where Kitty Martin was waiting, she could sense the bond between the two handsome people. The woman turned and ran lightly towards the car. She kissed her hands and called, 'See you tomorrow, darling.' She slammed the car door and started the engine and her blonde hair, held back by a chiffon scarf, blew out in a golden stream under the delicate blue material. She sent a flurry of gravel up from the wheels as she turned sharply. The man on the terrace watched her go and Kitty waited until he looked back at the home before she moved off on her moped.

The last thing she wanted just now was for him to see her dressed as she was and to recognise her. After seeing the throwaway elegance of the blonde girl, Kitty felt inadequate. She didn't even know if the moped would go.

Blue smoke came from the exhaust and she either had to go or to turn off the engine and pretend that she was coming back instead of leaving. The chances were that he hadn't seen her, being so intent on catching a last glimpse of the red sports car, and he wouldn't know who was in the uni-sex clothes and helmet. She glanced to see that no other vehicle was coming and drove slowly away, curving towards the terrace to leave the car park. She kept her eyes down as if looking for pot holes and when she looked in her rear-view mirror, she saw, to her horror, that the Commander was watching her intently, as if trying to place her. She saw his expression change. 'He's laughing at me!' she said, and put on speed.

She couldn't be sure if he knew who was on the bike, but he evidently thought that something was funny. It would be me, she thought glumly. It's always me.

The car ferry between East and West Cowes, although valuable as a link between two sides of the river Medina at its sea outlet, could never be described as a miracle of modern science. The flat platform on which cars and foot passengers streamed, by way of a lowered gangway of metal and wood, was drawn over the river by a system of chains and a labouring engine. In high summer and at rush hour, when the factories turned out the day shift, it was packed for each journey, and the queues grew longer and longer as the season progressed. On a spring afternoon, with the factories still working, there were only four cars waiting, plus a milk float and a lorry carrying fresh-smelling planks unloaded from a Scandinavian boat in one of the bays on the Medina.

The water eddied round the lowered ramp and the cars went aboard. Kitty loosened her helmet when she bought her ticket at the kiosk just clear of the tide line.

'Still driving that heap, Sister?'

She smiled, resignedly. The drawback to nursing in each of the Island hospitals from time to time during her stay on Wight, bringing her into contact with so many people scattered across the length and breadth of the area, was that she was constantly on her guard for just such a meeting with someone she had nursed or with a relative who had noticed her looking after a loved one. It was something which used to irritate her as a vague intrusion into her private life off duty, but she was now quite used to it and was philosophical about it.

'How's the back, Mike?' she asked.

'Misses your gentle touch, Sister. But mustn't grumble. I get by.'

She took her ticket and turned away, aware of the curious glances behind her as a party of four waited to buy tickets. She wheeled the bike to the side where a man in a very grubby dark blue Guernsey waved her into place. Oh, no! she thought. Why didn't I stay at Osborne and read a good book?

'Hello, Sister. Didn't know you in that lot. Want to buy a decent bike?'

'No, Sam, I'm happy with this one.' She laughed. 'It's been running ever since you mended it for me.' She stood back to let other vehicles take up position, but she was the last before the ramp went up. She hoped that Sam had other pressing duties, but he lounged by the rail, blocking her way to the metal stairs leading to the upper deck.

'Been away, Sister?' She nodded. 'Back now, though,' he said with the air of a man who really knows what he's talking about. 'Bet you missed us all.'

'You could say that. I like the Island in spring.'

'If you want any jobs done, my brother is on the

dole and he'd be glad to look over your bike or anything.'

'Thanks a lot, Sam. I'll know where to find you.' He grinned. 'I think I'll go up now.' She smiled. 'I like to see the river from this angle.'

'Still got that houseboat up the creek?' He laughed and looked round for an audience. 'Up the creek, Sister! looks like it an' all. You want my brother to paint that for you. Do a lovely job he would.'

'I'll let you know, but I might have to do it myself. I can't afford your brother just now, Sam.'

'Garn! He wouldn't rob you. Might put it on a bit for the nobs. Been scraping a bottom along near Osborne. Naval family along past the Queen's place. Nice house, nice boat, nice for some, Sister.' He pushed an oily rope aside and glanced over the side at two sailing dinghies making heavy weather in the tide. 'Where you working now?'

'At Osborne,' she said, hoping that this wasn't as public an announcement as it seemed. 'Very quiet at present, so I thought I'd go over and say hello to the Solent.'

'They had some Falklands wounded there, Sister. My auntie has a friend who works in the kitchen and they were ever so busy a little while ago.' She nodded, as if it was news to her. 'Lot of nice young ones, not like the usual lot after operations. Want to stay there for a bit, Sister. Just up your street, I'd say.'

'Sam!' She decided it was too late to go on the

deck now as the ramp was grating on the slipway. He moved forward to get the cars in line and she fixed her helmet safely again. A pair of high-heeled blue leather shoes came smartly down the stairs and Kitty realised that the woman who had been leaning over the rail listening to Sam was the blonde who had been with Surgeon Commander Roscoe. She stared at the young nursing sister and smiled. In spite of her growing awareness that this was the woman in the life of a man who was never far from her own thoughts, Kitty smiled, too. It was a good face, with something more than beauty, and if they had met in other working circumstances, she knew instinctively that they could have been friends. She bent her head over her machine, and Carol Gaynor stepped fastidiously past a patch of oil to her car. So I can't have the satisfaction of hating her, thought Kitty. She'd be perfect for any intelligent man.

The sea air was salty on her lips as she walked down to the promenade by the Royal Yacht Squadron, perhaps the most exclusive club in sailing circles. The small brass cannon stood in a gleaming row ready to fire salutes to royalty, to famous ships of the line and to give starting signals for racing. The strong smell of seaweed was as she remembered it from childhood, when her grandmother made her breathe deeply, convinced of the medicinal powers of the ozone it gave off. No amount of argument would ever shake her in this, nor would she admit that rotting seaweed was an unpleasant smell.

The front was deserted except for a row of children sitting on the ornate seats waiting for a coach to take them back to their own schools. Tennis gear told the story of a match played against the school further down towards Gurnard, and from the loud laughter, Kitty formed the opinion that they had won. But it made her look at her watch and realise that time was flitting by as she dreamed, looking out to sea and wondering what she might be doing in another year.

She went back to her moped and found to her relief that the chain ferry was filling up. She went on board and Sam was too busy to chat. She wondered where the sleek sports car had taken Carol Gaynor. She must either live on the Island or be staying with friends. Kitty frowned. Something about the woman made her think of her in a professional situation. Was she a doctor or a nursing sister? Strange how one member of a calling can recognise another. It could account for the slightly conspiratorial smile that passed between them when Sam was announcing to the world at large that one of his passengers was a nurse.

There was no sign of the sports car and the ferry had obviously been used as a short cut to the main Cowes-Newport road. The hill up towards the gates made the moped grunt and lose power and Kitty knew that soon she would have to trade it in for something a little more reliable.

The entrance to the Home was silent. Most of the residents would be resting before dinner or having tea in the sitting room. She changed back into uniform in the cloakroom, then went to find Sister Peggy Bowen who was going off for an evening and a day off.

'Hope the weather holds,' said Kitty Martin.

'I'm praying that it will. Mark is having trouble with an engine and we are taking it out for a trial.'

'Did you know that Captain Oliver is keen on marine engineering? He's still a bit down in the dumps but he should be moving well now he has to wear his foot for several hours a day.'

'That's an idea. We could do with another head and he couldn't come to any harm if we didn't depend on him for crew.' She smiled. 'Thanks for mentioning it. Mark wants to meet him and this will be the right way to do it.' She frowned. 'I wish I was as happy over the Lieutenant. Ever get the gut feeling that all is not well?'

'Too often.'

Sister Bowen frowned. 'Have you noticed anything? He tries to stay out of the way and keeps a stiff upper lip. Senior Service and all that jazz and lets us find out what he could tell us in five minutes.'

'He hates to admit that he's in pain, and who can blame him for putting off further surgery after all he's been through,' Kitty paused. 'But he is in pain. I saw him rubbing his leg and right thigh when he was on the terrace walking behind his chair for support.'

'And now he's back in bed, saying he's tired and doesn't want visitors. He's very firm about that, so please field them before they find him You did say the *right* side?' Kitty nodded. She had seen him facing the home and it was the side nearest to the stone beasts that gave him trouble. 'They took out several chunks of metal but the one they left was on the left side close to the spine. It's an ugly long sliver of steel that could move. They hope it will track along the muscle sheath and come to a spot where it is safe to go after it with as little effort and danger as possible.'

'Why didn't they do it all at once?' she asked.

'He had a bad entry wound and the others took too long. They cleaned up the debris and put him on anti-biotics. Now, they have to do something, if it moves in the wrong way.'

'But he has no fragments in his right side, now?'

'No . . . let's look at the X-rays again. This is an early one, taken when the metal fragments were still there. This is later, after the first op, showing the remaining one.'

They stared at the dark negatives displayed on the bright viewer, comparing the pictures and positions of the last fragment. 'I know it was the right side but there is no sign of damage on that side.'

'Where are his notes? I'll kill that house surgeon. He never gets his work done and he promised to sent them over with the pictures. Sometimes he holds data back for days.' She picked up her bag and looked at the time. 'Mark will be fuming. He's waiting to fetch me. Could you ring the naval hospital and ask for the notes—and there should be another batch of X-rays. I know they'll say they need to keep them for the next op, but we ought to monitor any deterioration.'

'I'll do that and I'll get him mobile tonight and note his reactions.'

'Good. Bruce Mycroft offered to play chess with him tonight, so if you hover, you might learn something, and I don't mean about Mycroft!'

'Have a nice evening. I'll start the medicine round and check on everyone now they are back inside,' Kitty said. She unlocked the drug cupboard and asked one of the nurses to check each drug before it was given, looking at the label and the name of the patient and measuring quantities. It was an aid to training auxiliaries and was a safe-guard to exclude any human error. There were not many dangerous drugs in circulation as drugs in this category were not necessary very often, but the Lieutenant was written up for a relaxant and a sleeping pill, neither of which he took unless in great pain, and in need of rest.

'Good evening,' she said when she entered the smoking room after dinner. 'Has everyone had evening medicines?'

Two men and a girl from Air Traffic Control who had been involved in a car accident nodded and said they needed nothing. Lt Commander Basil Sinclair pursed his lips and bent over the chess board, saying that he didn't need a sleeping pill.

'Shall I put one by your bed in case you need it later?' she asked.

'If I want anything, I'll ask the night nurse,' he said. He shifted in his chair as if very stiff and his hand wandered to his right thigh and hip.

'Is everything all right?' she asked in a low voice.

'Fine, Sister. I sat in a draught, I think. Bit of stiffness on this side.' He looked at her as if defying her to say it was anything more. 'It will work off. I'll take a turn along the corridor later.'

'I haven't taken your temperature today, Basil,' she said, gently. 'We ought to chart you while you are here.'

'In other words, you think I'm cooking up something sinister.' He smiled, wryly. 'Come off it, Sister. I do know the drill. I have a slight discomfort in my side and I know what caused it. End of diagnosis.'

'The night nurse can take it before you settle,' she said, ignoring his rising annoyance. She continued her round, glancing from time to time at the man who was physically fit but under great stress. The chiming clock struck in the hall and she wondered if she could get Basil to bed. He was pale and moved with extreme caution when he changed position in the chair. The men finished a game and she wanted to get him away before he suffered any embarrassment. He started when he heard the clock chiming.

'I think I'll go to my room,' he said. His colour was high. 'Can you come with me, Sister. You might as well do something useful instead of hovering over me as if I might drop dead at any minute.'

'Of course,' she said, with growing awareness that he needed help, but her training made her sound calm, as if she hadn't heard his sharp words. She wondered for a moment if the Commander was in pain? A vain hope, but it could account for some of his moods! It was completely out of character for Basil Sinclair to act like this. She brought a wheel-chair and he didn't refuse it. He stood in order to transfer to the chair and staggered. 'Damn,' he said through clenched teeth. Kitty lowered him into the chair and then beckoned a junior nurse. She whispered that Commander Roscoe must come to the Lieutenant's room and then pushed the chair slowly so that she couldn't jar his back. With gentle expertise, she helped him to sit on the bed while she took off his socks and trousers. Meekly he let her do so without protest and she found this more alarming than his burst of temper. She hastened to get him into clean poplin pyjamas.

'Could you prop me up more?' She saw that he rubbed his hip again.

'Is it worse?' He nodded, closing his eyes for a moment. 'Take this before I go,' she said, handing him the sedative. She wondered where the doctor could be.

'I'll take it if you'll stay for half an hour. If by that time I'm not better, you can send me to the mainland.'

'I ought to ring them now,' she said.

'First I must see Roscoe.'

Her heart sank. Where was the man? Out with

his blonde girl friend when one of his men needed him?

'Please, not yet. I want to see Roscoe. Go and give report or whatever you do now and then come back.'

Sister Martin went quickly to see the night sister and told her what was happening. The nurse came back from the tower where the resident doctor had rooms and she was out of breath. 'I can't find the Commander, Sister. I've looked in his office and in all the rooms, the dining room and the library. I rang the main block but the caretaker hasn't seen him and I can't think where to look now.'

'He must be here!' A chill spread over her. If he wasn't there, what could she do? Basil Sinclair needed help, and fast. The Commander was on call and had no right to be out with a woman, forgetting his duty. In spite of her resentment towards him, she knew that she was depending on him, and that the high opinion of his capabilities that the rest of the staff had was justified. He was a leader and a man who got things done. But where was he when she needed him?

She walked along the dimly lit corridor. The only place that hadn't been searched was the gym and pool. She saw a light under the door and went into the bright room. She blinked and saw him tying the belt of a bathrobe. His hair was wet and he looked more relaxed than she remembered.

'What the hell are you doing here? Can't a man

take a swim without being spied on?' He pulled the belt tighter.

'It's Basil Sinclair. We've been looking for you. He's in great pain and I think the metal in his back has shifted.' In her agitation, she put an urgent hand on his arm. 'Please come,' she said.

He looked down into her face and saw the trembling lips and great wide eyes. 'I'm coming,' he said, mildly. He bent to kiss her, and his eyes were sad. 'You're fond of the boy?' She nodded. Everyone was fond of Basil and hardly noticed his peculiar walk and the livid scars of the burns on his face as soon as he talked and smiled. 'Do you fall in love with all your patients?'

'No,' she said, drawing away. He grinned, and she knew that he was deliberately making her angry to make her put her thoughts in order.

'Better,' he said. 'Now, tell me symptoms if you've noticed any. Did the notes come from base?'

'No, I've rung about them and they will be here first thing tomorrow. I was very firm about it, Commander.'

'Good. Now, about Basil.' He went behind a screen and she saw the bathrobe flung over the top. In two minutes, he was with her again, wearing his track suit.

'He has the metal on the left but rubs his right hip and thigh and I think he's running a temp.'

'Hell!' He eased his shoulder as if it was stiff, then began to walk slowly to the door. She wanted to make him hurry. He might want time to think, but did he have to do it at a snail's pace? 'Go back and stay with him and ask Nurse to get the naval hospital on the buzzer,' he said.

She almost ran and when she got to the room where Basil lay, she was relieved to see that the drug was clouding the pain and he was drowsy.

'It's fine if I lie still. I think it's going away.' He looked up at her. 'I can't go to the mainland now. I have to see a lady tomorrow.'

'I didn't know you were expecting anyone.' There had been no mention of a booking for a meal with him, as was the custom if relatives came from a distance.

'She's staying locally.' He smiled. 'I saw her today, just for a minute. It was wonderful to see her again and she promised to come tomorrow.'

'Do I know her?' Anything to keep him talking so that he would be awake when the Commander came to examine him.

'I doubt it. Her name's Carol Gaynor and she's very pretty.'

'I didn't know you saw Carol.' They both looked towards the door, and Kitty wondered at the disapproval in the Commander's eyes. 'She looks great, but she wouldn't want to be worried by sickness just now, so it's up to you to co-operate to the full.' Basil flushed and his hands almost tore the bedcover. 'So you tell me exactly what's troubling you instead of waffling about a tiny niggle that will go away.'

Kitty stood watching and wondered, how hard can a man be? But it produced the required result. Basil seemed to pull his wits together and told them his symptoms. Gently, Kitty helped the sick man to lie on his front and exposed the scarred back. It was so like the scars she had glimpsed on the back of Surgeon Commander Alex Roscoe that she gasped. He looked at her sharply and his mouth became a grim line. He traced the old wound edges and found the slight bulge that indicated where the metal lay. Kitty held the latest X-ray up to the light and knew that the metal was now close to the vital centres of the spine.

'Back to the knife, old boy, and quickly,' said the Commander.

'Not tomorrow. If she goes away, I may never see her. I couldn't face it tomorrow.'

'And do you think she will want to see you in pain? Are you so selfish that you think a woman can love you when you are not whole? Even Sister Martin flinches when she sees your scars.'

'No! That's not true,' she whispered, appalled by the bitterness of his face.

'And Carol isn't ready for shocks from any of us.'

Kitty wanted to run out. Couldn't he pretend that Carol might spare some love for Basil even if she was in love with the stronger of the two men? It would do no harm to let him dream just for a while until he recovered his physical strength and his pride.

'He's had a pill?' he asked.

'Yes, Commander.'

'Remove his drinking water and put a notice in the kitchen that he is to have no food,' he said as soon as the door closed behind them. 'I have to ring the hospital again. They missed this one,' he said, savagely, 'and unless we want a paraplegic we have to act.'

'That bad?'

'I think so. I diagnose Brown Séquard syndrome. We had one after soldiers were playing silly B's with live ammunition on Salisbury Plain last year, and a bullet lodged in the nerve above the lumbar spine. He ached and was cold on the side away from the lesion. Mostly motor responses affected but also some sensation lost.'

'Was he all right?'

'With luck he may walk in two years.'

'Oh, *no*!'

He caught her in his arms. 'Don't look like that for him. He doesn't need you.' He kissed her fiercely, then smiled. 'That, Sister Martin, is thank you for your correct observation and speedy diagnosis.'

'Please stop making fun of me.'

He gently stroked her face, and smiled. 'Don't look so annoyed. If you hadn't told me about him, by tomorrow, we might have been too late.'

'What are you going to do?'

She heard the drone of a helicopter above the lawn. 'That is what we must do. They are alerted in the mainland and he'll go straight to theatre.'

'He won't see his visitor?'

'I shall see her,' he said. 'I can explain.'

He was right. Of course he was right, but he was cruel and hard and would steal a man's hopes. She walked quickly away to pack a bag for Basil to take. And that kiss . . . a throwaway gesture as one might smooth the head of a pet. What woman needed that?

The next half hour was too full for personal thoughts and it was late before she could leave the Home. She went out into the cold night air. The seat of her moped was damp and the engine took a long time to start. The garage must have patched it up and delivered it with no great hopes that it would serve her well. She had forgotten to buy bread and the pull of the vehicle told her that its days were numbered. That's all I need, she told herself. And tomorrow, she might have to watch Alex Roscoe mooning over his lovely blonde. The memory of his kiss cooled in the night mist, his grip lost its impact but her heart held a treasure. It had been an almost contemptuous kiss, but one that made it impossible for her to take Paul as a lover.

CHAPTER FOUR

SISTER Kitty Martin shaded her eyes and looked up at the sky. The morning was bright and the light cloud showed no sign of coming rain. It was silly to look up at the sky and hope the helicopter would return with Commander Roscoe in it. Last night, she had worried about him. He was so relaxed after swimming that she began to wonder if he had been as stiff as some of the other men who had suffered similar wounds in the Falklands campaign. She recalled the deep scars on his back and knew that he also had a little more metal in his muscles which might or might not have to be removed at some future date.

He was sensitive about his appearance. That at least was becoming clear. One or two little incidents added up to a picture of a man who had been a perfect specimen of humanity and now felt at a disadvantage. Except with Carol, the lovely girl who so obviously adored him and to whom he gave his sweetest smiles. It was vanity on a big scale. If he had Carol and didn't mind bearing his scars to her, then he had no need to bother with outsiders. Why couldn't men believe that women loved some sign of weakness in the strongest of men? I would love him even if he was disfigured, she admitted to herself. She caught her breath. 'Stop looking like him,' she scolded the sardonic-looking carved beast on the terrace.

He certainly wasn't disfigured, and his movements were loosening up each time she saw him. The slight limp that he tried to hide by staying still whenever he saw her was so slight that she would never have noticed it if his efforts to hide it had not brought it to her attention.

She went into the office. The night staff were ready to go and had little to report. 'You had all the excitement,' they said.

'Any news about Basil?'

'They found the metal and removed it. He'll be in a plaster bed for a while to let the inflammation die down but will be lifted out for physio as soon as they know there is no lasting damage.' The girl smiled. 'The Commander is staying for two days, so any calls go to the civilian locum in the town.'

'I didn't know he had leave?'

'I think he assisted last night and met some friends. He rang through and asked if you would ring later at this number in case there was mail for him.'

'Why me? The porter could do that.'

'He said you, so perhaps he doesn't mind if you read his mail.' She laughed. 'He also said that if a lady calls, to explain where he is and to ask her to go over to see him.'

Kitty frowned. Was this an excuse to be away from prying eyes and to have the lovely girl to himself for two nights? She could visit him at Osborne, but it was bad for discipline if she stayed as his guest.

The day started quietly, with Bruce Mycroft following her as she did her round, subdued and helpful, without the bombastic air that he usually wore when women were around or he wanted to impress. 'You come up for the board in a few days, don't you?' she asked, suddenly aware that he needed some kind of comfort.

'Do you think I'll go back as AI?' He touched the healed burns on his neck and chin.

'You can have grafts first or you can leave it for a few months and go off sick again once you are back. No problem as far as I can see. You are mobile and really need more exercise now that you are up. You could lose a little weight.'

'Is that all?'

'You're out of condition and you aren't like that as a rule, are you?' He looked at her seriously. 'If a man is out of condition for whatever reason, he is slightly breathless and clumsy.'

'Right.'

'If you swim and use the gym before you go before the board, I don't think you have a problem.' She glanced at him shrewdly. 'You also need to see more people outside this place. Take off that very dashing scarf that you wear tucked in to hide the scars, and flaunt them.'

He reddened. 'I'm sorry. I do all the wrong things.'

'If you think that chasing the nurses, who have seen it all, will give you a lift, do so by all means. We treat it as an occupational hazard and it makes it more difficult when you leave here.'

He hovered in the doorway of her office and she took pity on him and offered him coffee when her own tray arrived. The telephone rang, and she was glad he was there. For some reason, she didn't want to be alone when Carol Gaynor rang. She braced herself and spoke normally.

'Could I speak to Commander Roscoe? Tell him his sister is here,' a strange voice said.

'I'm sorry, but the Commander is away. Can I take a message? We shall be in contact soon by telephone.' She remembered the number that she was to give Carol. What did it matter if his sister broke up his weekend love nest? 'I do have a number here if you would like it. He's on the mainland after taking a patient to the naval hospital last night.'

'Damn.' The voice had a certain resemblance to the voice that she knew so well. It was low and forthright and Kitty imagined a female version of the tall, dark and imposing Commander. 'Has he seen Carol? You have met Carol? I was hoping to see her.'

So it was accepted in the family that where the Commander was, there would be the lovely blonde.

'I have to give her a message if she calls,' Kitty said.

'Would you tell her that Blanche Roscoe called and that I shall be staying in one of the guest rooms here as soon as I get settled.' She sighed. 'Annoying. I hate kicking my heels waiting for people and if Alex isn't there, I'm wasting time. I am seeing friends in East Cowes and they want me to go sailing, but I had hoped to see Alex today. Is he having his back done soon?'

'His back? I thought he had finished surgery.'

'Only a local to take out splinters as they come to the surface I believe, and he wanted one of the scars trimmed and straightened. A bit of a cobbler's job, don't you think?'

'I wouldn't know, Miss Roscoe.'

'And he wouldn't show you.' She laughed. 'My brother is marvellous. He makes everyone do as he says and yet he does exactly as he likes in spite of expert advice. I bully him as much as I can, but he should have a strong-minded wife to keep him in order.'

'I can't imagine him being kept in order by anyone.'

Blanche Roscoe chuckled. 'You said that with feeling. What is your name? I'd like to meet you when I come to the Home.'

Kitty told her and gave her the telephone number. As she rang off, the phone rang again. This time it was Carol. Bruce Mycroft sat drinking coffee and made no attempt to hide his curiosity. Kitty wondered what he gathered from the one-sided conversations. Carol seemed upset to hear that Basil Sinclair had been taken away as an emergency. She hesitated and said that she would write a note and leave it for the Commander in the office as she had to go away. 'I'll send some flowers for Basil,' she said, and Kitty wondered how she could be so casual about men who both adored her and needed her with them. Even if she was not in love with Basil, it was an act of common humanity to visit him when he was ill.

'But the Commander is away today,' Kitty said.

'Give it to him when he comes. I have to go now.'

She was staying within walking distance of the home and yet she was going to send a note.

'You can't stay there all day,' Kitty told Mycroft. 'I have work to do. Why not get some exercise this morning and I could take out the boat this afternoon. Do you sail?'

'I did, once.' His face cleared. 'It might be what I need. I'll ask the boy who is due for discharge to lend us some muscle, if that's all right.'

'Fine. I'll see you after lunch.'

The morning went on and she had no opportunity to ring the number at the naval hospital. She went into her office while the residents were eating and as she sat down to use the telephone, she saw the small pile of mail addressed to the Commander. One envelope had been delivered by hand and she knew at once that it was from his lady love. Slowly, she raised the phone and got the number. She frowned. It was the main number of the hospital, and the voice answering asked if she was enquiring for a patient.

'I'd like to know how Lieutenant Sinclair is. He came to you from Osborne last night when I was on duty.'

'Oh, you're staff! He's going to be fine. Better than he was after the first op and it will be only a matter of days. Once the sliver of metal was out, the relief was immediate, but he still felt weak.'

'I really wanted to speak to the Commander.'

'Ah, yes, he assisted last night and stayed on.' The voice paused. 'Yes, you can speak to him now. I'll put you through.'

Almost as if he was a patient, too, thought Kitty. I suppose we all get like that. She heard his voice and her heart seemed to lurch.

'This is Sister Martin,' she began.

'You took your time,' he said. His voice was tired and she knew that he must have been up for most of the night. But it was now nearly one o'clock. He could have slept for hours since the op, so she didn't waste sympathy on him.

'I've been busy, Commander. I'm sorry if you wanted a call earlier but your mail has just arrived.'

'Tell me,' he said in a bored voice.

She read out post marks and said which were official communications of a routine nature. He told her to put them on one side. She took up the pale pink envelope. 'One by hand, and I think it is from your friend. She rang earlier to say she couldn't see you today. Your sister rang, too. She is staying with friends in East Cowes.'

'Yes, I know about her. She rang. Open the letter.'

'I could send it on when the launch goes over tonight. It might be private.'

'Read it,' he ordered.

She opened the letter, reluctantly. The paper was thick and deckle-edged and the envelope was lined with dark red. She unfolded the single sheet. 'My darling Alex', it began. 'I think it *is* personal,' she said.

'Go on, read it.'

'My darling Alex, by the time you receive this, I shall be away. I know it is sudden but I have no option. The opportunity came and I had to take it. I know you will understand that this is an opportunity I couldn't miss. I would like to have seen Basil and you, and it would have been good to have you with me on this trip, but when I face our friends on Blue Beach, I shall be with a lot of people I know. My best love as always, Carol.'

'I see. So she has gone after all.' His tone was heavy, and Kitty was filled with fury against the beautiful girl who couldn't face suffering. It was very nice to be able to join a group on some far flung beach where she would meet old friends, but had she thought of the disappointment that Basil would suffer if he was told that she had left without seeing him?

He made no comment about the letter. 'I told my

sister to go up to the Home and make herself useful until I get back tomorrow. She can push a few chairs and use the pool, so make her work, Sister. I shall check on Sinclair and be back tomorrow evening. Blanche can have dinner with me in my quarters.'

'Will that be all, Commander?'

'You *could* have dinner with us and make her feel welcome.' He laughed and it was more normal. 'I suppose you do have other clothes?'

'Other than uniform?'

'That and those incredible pants and helmet.'

'Of course. I have sailing clothes and church clothes and clothes for evenings out with people. I even have overalls for when I clean out my boat.'

'Don't wear them. Just something crisp,' he said, dismissing her. She had no time to refuse and she shrugged as she left the office to change for the afternoon.

The breeze was slight and she wondered if it was worth the effort to get the boat trimmed, but one glance at the two eager men told her that they were ready for anything to break the boredom. Bruce Mycroft seemed much nicer when he forgot his forthcoming board, and the subaltern beamed with excitement.

'Home on Saturday, Don?' she asked. He nodded. 'Well, we'll try not to drown you first.'

He carried some of the gear that wasn't stored in the boat house and Kitty found his efforts welcome.

The breeze strengthened and Bruce said there would be fun in the Solent. 'Are you sure you want to bother with me?' he asked, and she began to wonder if he regretted coming.

'I've been looking forward to trying the dinghy,' she said. 'This is too good a chance with all your muscle to help.'

Don was only too eager to get started. 'You look fine,' she said, noting that Bruce's throat was bare and that the scars showed plainly, as if he wanted to try exposing them to her and Don before letting anyone else see them. And they say that women worry about their looks, she thought!

'I still feel awkward,' he admitted.

'Miss Roscoe will be visiting. You can show yourself to her. With such a brother, she must be used to seeing patients.'

'He used to talk about her sometimes.' He blushed and the scars showed red. 'I don't know if I'm all that keen on meeting her. Alex suggested it before he got fed up with me assing around, and I wanted to do so, but now, I don't think it would work. Not a good idea,' he said, throwing his bag on to the deck. 'No woman would want to sit with me for an evening unless I wore a scarf. As for anything more, it's laughable.'

'Just forget it now. Go on from today and take it as it comes. People will like you because you have interests in common. After half an hour talking, I never notice the colour, size or status of people if they are pleasant and interesting.'

'You are a sweetie. I bet your boy friend adores you.'

'I haven't a boy friend. I am married to my work,' she said, laughing. She tossed extra sweaters on board with a cushion or two in case one of the men ached in odd places. After all, they were still under medical supervision.

'Alex said that, too.'

'He did? How could he know?'

'He said that any woman who made the effort to come to work on that terrible moped must be so devoted to her job that she couldn't stay away.'

'I had no idea that I was discussed,' she said, and blushed. 'I shall fool you all soon. I shall come to work in a brand-new second-hand car, and be able to emerge beautiful and serene like other women.'

'Don't change. We like you as you are,' he said, and bent to tie a sailing shoe.

Out in the Solent, a huge liner passed on the sky line, steaming out of Southampton harbour on the way to America. The ship was already passing from sight away on the horizon, but the wash that came minutes after it left came rolling in. A wave slapped against the boat and sent spray over the bow, a cabin cruiser tipped and emerged from the swell to the right of the shoreline, a sand dredger ploughed solidly through the waves, tossing off water that came over the hull, and a speed boat twisted to come bows on to ride the wash.

The scene was a crazy mixture of near disaster and control, with spent waves being hurled back to mingle in confusion, with more waves coming on to the sand. A giant hand shook with rage under the water, threatening and playing with whatever came its way. Kitty stood back to watch, admiring the white foam and the sheer strength of the water.

'Quite a sight, isn't it? In summer, the wash never fails to catch holiday makers who leave their gear too close to the water. They watch the boats and the wash and don't realise that it comes in so much.' She turned to Bruce. 'What's wrong?'

He sat on the sands with his face in his hands. 'It's no use. I can't go.'

'It will be calm soon. Look! the waves are getting smaller and the white crests have gone. I doubt if we shall have wind enough for a sail.'

'No,' he said in a broken voice. 'It's like it was out there. The waves and the chaos.'

Kitty sat on the beach beside him and Don moved away. 'Look,' she said, gently. As if some miracle had touched the water, it was calm and the sun sent silvery tips to cover the waves, making it look warmer than it was. 'You needn't go today, but watch it and see that there is no fire.'

He stared at the calm sea. 'You know that Alex was there when they fished me out?' She shook her head. 'I went into a blazing sea and we were picked up by inflatables. Alex came to give us morphine as most of us had burns and when I got on board, he was there, working the clock round in the theatre.' He gave a short laugh. 'He saved many lives that night, and at dawn went on deck for a breather. There was another batch waiting.'

'And then?' Kitty willed him to go on. This was no 'once upon a time' and the man had to re-live it to wash it from his mind. It was the first time that she had heard about Alex in the Falklands.

'A mortar shell fell aft and killed a man. Splinters of metal went everywhere and Alex got some. Basil Sinclair got his there too, but much worse. Alex thought it funny that he should end up on the table he had been using for so many hours. He refuses to admit it, but he's a bloody hero.'

'So are you all,' she said, softly. 'Not least now when you have painful memories.' She touched his throat that lay bare in the sunlight. 'It wasn't this that bothered you. Come sailing and then you can tell the assessment board that you can face the sea.'

'Hi there! Can anyone join?' The slim dark girl came down the path to the shore. 'It was too nice an afternoon to waste reading, and I couldn't hang about Cowes all day.'

'Miss Roscoe?'

'You don't mind? I wanted to find out about Basil but there doesn't seem to be any further news.'

'We were just thinking about sailing, but that's as far as we got. We may put it off again. I'm Kitty Martin and this is Bruce Mycroft, and that's Don.'

He raised a hand and shouted that everything

was on deck and when could he cast off? 'What are you doing, wasting fair weather and good sailing time?'

'Fine,' said Blanche Roscoe. 'I didn't bring sailing shoes but I can roll up my trousers and go bare foot. Nice to meet you, Bruce. Alex told me a lot about you. I expected to see Dracula!'

Kitty laughed and the two women exchanged glances.

'Go sailing much?'

Bruce looked at the girl who gazed directly into his face without seeming to see anything unusual. 'Trying to make up for lost opportunities,' he said. He gulped and looked at Kitty for help. 'Do we go now?'

'Give a hand, Don. You first, Miss Roscoe, then Bruce, and I'll cast off and try to keep my feet dry.'

'Call me Blanche. Can't stand protocol. All this service stuff makes me want to throw up.'

Bruce looked at her as if she was a mermaid he had caught in his net and Kitty saw that she was beautiful. Like her brother in the dark hair and grey eyes, the firm chin and the athletic build, but while he was the epitome of masculine sexuality, she had more than her fair share of feminine attraction. Colour came back to Bruce's face and he no longer clutched at the metal stay as if he might fall overboard.

The breeze held and they sailed along to the opening to Wootton Creek before turning back to

Osborne. Kitty explained that she lived on a house-boat there, far up by the bridge and road but away from all land dwellings. 'It's very convenient when I'm working on the Island,' she said.

'It has to be,' said Bruce. 'You should see the way she rides that awful bike. Quicker to walk.'

'Or sail. I have sailed over to Osborne once or twice, but only when I've the time. Tides and winds round here are unreliable and I wouldn't do it even in a speed boat as routine.'

Blanche took the tiller and seemed to be enjoying herself. Bruce had regained his humour and was teasing them.

'Believe it or not, I'm off duty,' said Kitty, severely. 'I give up my free time to a man who insults me and then I have to go back and change into uniform and treat him kindly because he is a patient.'

They tied up and removed the sails to the locker. 'Thank you for bringing me,' said Bruce, like a child given an orange and a balloon when leaving a party, but his eyes were serious and Kitty knew what an effort it had been to come to terms with the water again. One more hurdle over. She wondered when Alex Roscoe would give up thinking that he even had a hurdle to cross.

The two men were tired and Kitty handed them over to a nurse with strict instructions that they rest before dinner. She went for coffee before changing back into uniform for the evening, and Blanche went to get her gear so that she could settle into the guest house.

No wonder I haven't heard of Blanche before now. Who would have imagined that his sister would be an Air Stewardess on a famous airline? And she was so easy to know, Kitty thought.

'I have two weeks leave,' Blanche had said, 'but I can extend it.' She had looked at Bruce as he walked away into the building. 'He'll make it,' she said. 'Thought he'd pass out when he got on board but he will be fine now. I might even help him along a bit. Is it true that he went through a phase when he was pretty bloody-minded?' Kitty nodded. 'I know the feeling. Alex hates to be sick and thinks the gods have a personal grudge if he has to suffer. He'll do, too,' she said, and gave Kitty a long cool look that made her redden. Blanche gave a reflective smile. 'Alex and I can't help organising people. Just wait. Alex has it all worked out and I think I have, too.'

Which means he is all set to marry the lovely Carol Gaynor, I suppose, Kitty thought. She did the evening round and missed Basil very much. She remembered that he used the room in the tower where the telescope was situated and sometimes left library books there. Everyone was occupied, and Bruce was half asleep on a chaise longue, so she went up to the tower and collected the books and some writing paper Basil used. The lights from vessels out in the Channel blinked in the darkness and she looked through the glass at the stars. It was clear and bright out there with no sorrow, no hangups, and she knew how Basil found peace in this room. She looked down and saw a large car sweep into the drive and for a moment thought it might belong to Alex Roscoe, but he was alone on the mainland without the woman who should have met him there but deserted him when the whim took her to America to meet other people on a beach somewhere.

She wondered what to wear for dinner the following night. He had asked her as female company for his sister and out of politeness because she had been useful. It would serve him right if I did wear my moped gear, she thought, smiling, but was already planning her clothes in detail. There was no hope of attracting him away from Carol Gaynor, but as a matter of pride, she wanted to show that she could look very good when she gave her mind to dressing. Tomorrow, she would look at the car that Sam's brother had lined up for her inspection and another that she had seen advertised in the local press. She hummed to herself as she locked up the drug cupboard and put away the notes.

There was only report to write and she could go home. Off duty in the morning and having dinner after duty at night with the one man who had taken over her heart! And once upon a time, I didn't even like him, she thought. Knowing Blanche helped her understanding of the proud and incredibly handsome man. It was as if he might be as frank and humorous as his sister if he was in the mood and with the right company. It was useless to hope and to dismiss his involvement with Carol Gaynor as a passing fancy, but there was no law against wanting to be with him and enjoying his company at a time when he wouldn't be so impolite as to bawl her out for something.

She answered the telephone twice. Relatives had a habit of ringing after dinner at night and the calls were put through to the bedrooms. During the day, so many of the convalescent officers were scattered over the house and grounds and difficult to locate in time to answer calls, that this had become the time for telephoning. It rang again and she started. 'Sister Martin here,' she said.

'Sister? Who the hell has been on this line? I've been trying to get through to you for the past half hour.'

It was as bad as she remembered it, with his voice hard and tense, as if she was personally responsible for all the incoming calls to Osborne.

'Some of the relatives ring during the evenings, as you know, Commander.' She kept her tone light. 'What can I do for you?'

'Do? Nothing. They could do with you here in this very busy hospital instead of you wasting your time on people almost ready to go home. But I suppose it is a soft option.'

'That's not fair,' she said. 'I do all kinds of nursing and go where I'm sent.'

'I'm sorry.' He seemed to be making an effort.

'It's just that I couldn't get through to you and I rang my friends in East Cowes to see if my sister was there and they have all gone out to the West Wight.'

'Can I help? Or you could ring her later.'

'Thank you.' The words were forced. 'If you could ask her to ring here tomorrow morning early?'

'Certainly, Commander. I'll leave a note in the guest house on my way home tonight.'

She hesitated, unsure if she now wanted to have dinner with him the following evening. He was so cutting and seemed to be very tense. Perhaps he had been working too hard and was now stiff and uncomfortable after assisting at Basil's operation. She sighed, softly. Much more likely was the thought that he was pining for Carol Gaynor and had to vent his frustration on someone.

'You sighed?' His voice softened. 'I'm a bad-tempered bastard. I had a lot to do tomorrow and now I shall be otherwise engaged. I wanted to say that I have to cancel our dinner date tomorrow. Tell Blanche to come over to see me here instead. It's time she saw Basil again. He needs cheering up.'

'I'll tell her,' she said.

'Sorry about dinner. Some other time, perhaps.'

'Perhaps.'

She stared at the dead phone. And perhaps not. It was so blatantly obvious that he couldn't stand her company and this was a clumsy way out of having to be reasonably polite to the Sister who was good at her job but only fit for a little slap and tickle with the bored patients.

'Time to go home, Kitty,' she said. 'Time to go home and take a long cool look at your life.'

CHAPTER FIVE

THE influx of new patients was over and the staff had sorted out notes and assigned them to the various remedial sessions appropriate to their individual needs. Sister Kitty Martin felt as if the convalescent home was at last returning to its peacetime role, as most of the men and women involved in the Falklands war had left for the last time, either home or back to their units.

It was good to be busy once more, to have little time to think and to stick to normal off duty, living a life outside the stately residence and away from the peace and insidious charm of Osborne. It was nearly a week since Basil Sinclair had gone into hospital and there had been little to report as he was making an uneventful recovery. Blanche Roscoe had seen him and had little to add to the official reports, but on the subject of her brother she was strangely reticent. She saw Kitty sometimes but spent most of her time with Bruce Mycroft and with friends who lived a short distance along the coast from Osborne House. Once, Kitty had seen her out in a very fine yacht with two people and Bruce announced with pride that he had been sailing with them, too.

He was pathetically grateful to her for breaking

the chain of mental horror he suffered about the sea, and she tried to find consolation in the fact that she did her work well and that *some* people liked her. She was needed for her professional care but she knew that if she was to be happy, she must plot out a future in which Commander Roscoe had no part.

He had been away now for several days and the visiting locum said nothing about his return. Seeing Blanche was no help. For one thing, she was vague about him returning and, for another, she was an acute reminder of his forceful charm. The way she held her head when deciding something, and the sudden smile, was so much like her brother.

'Basil is coming out soon?' Kitty ventured one day when they were having coffee together.

'He's going to stay with the people in East Cowes. It's an enormous house and he knows them well. Carol will be there, too, so we'll have quite a party.' Blanche blushed. 'Bruce Mycroft might pay them a visit if he gets leave after his assessment.'

'I thought you were going back. How does the air service operate without you?' Kitty tried to joke but it was increasingly difficult.

'I'm taking more leave now. We had a mad scramble earlier when half the cabin staff on our route had Hong Kong trots and all leave was cancelled so that the aircraft could be staffed. Like nurses, we are expected to be super-human and are looked on as less than the dust if we have so much as a sniff.'

'I know the feeling. You also have to look after sick passengers, so you need some nursing expertise.'

Blanche stood up and looked at her watch. 'Bruce wanted to go for a long walk to loosen up his legs for tomorrow. Tomorrow, of course, being the day he dreads and longs for.'

'He has you to thank for a lot,' said Kitty.

'You, too. Between us we've sorted him out,' said Blanche, cheerfully. 'If only all men would give a little and not object to being spoiled.' She laughed. 'I can't talk. I'm like that. I back into a hole and snarl at anyone who wants to help me.' She gave Kitty a level glance. 'Alex is even worse,' she said. 'But you have probably gathered he isn't easy.'

'He is, with Carol Gaynor.'

'Of course,' said Blanche and smiled as she walked away.

Kitty finished her coffee. Even Blanche seemed to find no fault with the girl who had suddenly left her friends to go to America. Basil might have died or been paralysed for life after this last operation; any woman with any heart would have stayed at least for a few days, even if she didn't love him. Perhaps she was with Alex Roscoe now, making him leave his duties to take her somewhere now that she was back from America. She frowned. Blanche had mentioned that she would be staying in East Cowes when Basil went there. I suppose he will look besotted and forgive her anything, while she makes huge sheeps' eyes at the Commander, she thought.

She went home, feeling more and more excluded from the tight little circle and wondering if it might be wise to ask her agency to find her work in another hospital.

The houseboat came in for a lot of furious spring cleaning to take her mind off the man who had shattered the calm of her existence. The deck was freshly varnished and the wheel house shone with effort and new white paint and Kitty wondered if it might be a good idea to get the out-of-work brother of the man on the chain ferry to help her with the rest of the painting. It wasn't because she was sorry for him. She wasted no sympathy in that direction. He did very well out of 'moonlighting' and was better off than if he had been in full employment.

The moped had decided that it was time to go where all defunct vehicles go, and the rather good second-hand car filled Kitty with relief that never again would she have to wear lumpy clothes and a crash helmet unless she chose to do so. As she walked to the car park, she waved to Bruce who was unloading a case from his car. 'I like you better on a bike,' he taunted her.

'Good sailing?' she said.

'Fantastic! I have you and Blanche to thank for that. I sent for some decent clothes so that I can go about more easily. I can't leave here looking scruffy.' He looked serious. 'I know I shall never be the Adonis I was, but everything is slotting in again and it's wonderful.'

'I'm sad that you'll be going soon.'

'I'll come and see you, Sister Kitty.'

'Do that,' she said, but as she drove along to the junction and turned off for Wootton, she doubted if he'd bother to visit her once he was perfectly fit. There was so little she knew about him, about Blanche and about the set-up with Alex Roscoe and Carol. Perhaps even Blanche knew nothing about her own brother and his love life. If they were so alike, it was possible that he kept his affairs to himself with the same reticence that Blanche used when trying not to discuss her brother.

Kitty overtook a van that wavered in the middle of the road. They had a circle into which she would never have entrée. Blanche must know Carol very well if they had such close mutual friends. She frowned. It seemed odd that she never mentioned her except in passing, but was it surprising that she was excluded from confidences if they thought she had no place with them?

The soft evening was all spring colour, a kind of watercolour in greens and yellows. Kitty recalled the primroses in the copse by the Creek and wondered if they were there again this year. Primroses were a part of growing up. Her grandmother would pick them each year, saying that they were the favourite flowers of the Queen. Kitty smiled. Even generations on from Victoria, she was still the Queen who had lived at Osborne and had given her blessing to the Primrose League of Victorian politics.

She parked by the boat and walked up the gangway. The soft light across the water from houses high on the banks was broken by a stronger light inside the cabin. Paul heard her coming and poked his head outside. 'Hello, the door was propped open, so I walked in.'

'I hope you didn't smudge my paint!' She looked cross. 'It took me ages to do that. You've more on your jeans than I have on my door.'

He strolled past her to look at the car and leaned on the rail. 'This isn't wet, too, is it?'

'No, not that, but the locker there is still tacky. I wish you'd stay still. You make me nervous. I have a feeling that I am going to have to re-paint almost everything after you've been here for five minutes.'

'I'll be careful.'

'It's too late now. I took ages to get the right gloss on that surface.'

She didn't know why she was going on about it, having decided to employ a man to finish it, but all her bottled-up bad temper erupted.

'All right, I'll come and help if you want me to.'

'It isn't that. Just look at your clothes.'

'Not to worry.' He made ineffective dabs at the paint stains on his trousers.

'I'm not worrying about you. Just don't transfer any to the rest of the boat.' She spread a dust sheet on the large divan that doubled as a day time settee. 'Sit there and behave.'

'I could take them off, if you're that fussy.' He regarded her with a half smile. 'Work getting a drag? Could have told you it would. Not the nice good-tempered Kitty-cat I love.' She gave him a look. 'Don't be like that. I hoped you'd cook for me.'

'I am not cooking tonight. I can't eat with the smell of paint everywhere. I'm going out.' It was almost a surprise to her, as she had made no plans for the evening, but suddenly, the sight of Paul with three days stubble and filthy jeans made her want to tell him to go away and not come back.

'OK. I'll pretty myself and pick you up in half an hour.' He swung out, missing the paint by inches. 'Bye for now.'

'Paul?'

But he had gone and she was left with a date she didn't want and hadn't asked to have. She touched the tacky paint and wondered just when did people manage to get a door dry unless they moved out for a week? She had painted it before going on duty that morning and it was only touch dry. It was no use asking Paul to help. He had a built-in allergy to manual labour and anything that didn't concern his own research and his appetite.

Slowly she changed into a mohair sweater of rich green and a pair of smooth velvet jeans that echoed the colour. Thankfully, she released the tight pleat in which her hair was confined for duty and sent it shimmering down in a curve on to her shoulders. It felt good and she regained some of her cool.

'Ready?'

She looked up at Paul who now stood on the deck regarding the offending door with suspicion. She laughed. He looked quite different, with a clean-shaven jaw, brushed hair and a new sweat-shirt of tan and blue over good trousers. His pleasant face was smiling and he was very pleased with himself.

'Come on, I'm taking you out for a meal,' he said.

'They won't know you along the road if you go in looking clean!'

'We're not going there. There's a new place on an old ferry anchored off-shore in the creek. No, we don't have to paddle, it's quite civilised.'

'I heard about that.' Kitty regarded him with suspicion. 'It's quite pricy, too. I thought you were in a permanent state of penury.'

'I had a bit of luck. They gave me an advance on that text book I compiled and they kept for so long.' He grinned. 'They want some more and showed interest in the latest effort which has nothing to do with the text-book subject, so they know I'm not just a pair of painty jeans.'

'I'm thrilled for you, Paul.' She smiled, her genuine pleasure showing. 'You work very hard in your own way and sometimes I suppose you must get depressed about it.'

'No. I do work I like, and if they don't want it, well they can do the other.'

'You'll never be rich.'

'I'm on my way. They begin to see the real genius behind this brave façade.'

His car was by the water but he steered her towards her own.

'I thought you were taking me,' she said.

'You supply the transport. I might want to get pissed.'

'Thanks very much! But I suppose you now have white paint over your seats?'

'I covered them as I had my best knickers on.'

She opened the car and he sat beside her, still smiling. Her heart lurched with a kind of love that had no relationship to the intense feeling she had for Alex Roscoe. This man inspired liking and irritation and a fondness that made him precious in a way, but she was sad to think that he might want her more than she could ever want him.

The darkening hedgerows made solid barriers to the night as they made their way down the narrow lane to the restaurant. Music came fitfully as doors were opened and shut, and cars switched off headlights. Groups of men and women in smart but casual clothes went into the main reception area and small lamps lit the balconies made from the upper deck of the original ferry. Kitty laughed. 'The chain ferry at Cowes could look like this with a spot of paint.'

'I doubt it,' said Paul. He turned to the head waiter. 'Yes, I rang earlier.'

Kitty raised her eyebrows. Paul was such a mixture. He had already booked a table for them

before they met and yet he had come to the boat
looking as he did, as if to test her reactions and
mood. If I liked him as he was, he might think I
shall be rather more pliable tonight. She regarded
him anew. Several times she had sensed that hard
edge of calculation when he wanted his own way.
More subtle than Blanche, but as determined, she
decided. He led her to the table and she began to
enjoy the evening. The long day dissolved into food
and wine and music and the company of a man who
was easy, and, now that he was elated about his
success, very entertaining.

She smiled at him over the low candle holder and
wondered if life with him would be impossible. I
can't have the man I want, so why not Paul? He put
a hand over hers and smiled, willing to wait for the
right moment. She drew her hand away and knew
that she was deceiving herself. She glanced away
from his intense eyes and saw Carol Gaynor sitting
at a table a few yards away with a man.

'Seen someone you know?' Paul swung round.

'No, I don't know her. She was a visitor at the
convalescent home.' He turned back, and Kitty
bent over her plate.

'Thought you'd seen a ghost. Is she with one of
your patients?'

'No. I've never seen him.' Something about the
man was vaguely familiar. She had been in the
room where the telescope was kept for viewing the
sea and had taken a clearer look at the yacht that
came into sight. The man at the next table was the

same as the man at the helm, but this time he was dressed in a dark blazer and well-cut slacks instead of the sawn-off jeans he wore sailing. It tied up with the fact that Carol Gaynor had friends close to Osborne, and that Blanche knew these people too.

'You seem fascinated by that couple.' Paul sounded curious.

'No, I was just wondering about their connection with one of the residents at Osborne.'

'Which one?'

'He's not there now,' she said, quickly. 'I doubt if I shall see him again.'

'But you want to know about him?'

'No, of course not. Just professional interest as he had to go back for further surgery.'

Paul half rose to his feet. 'You could ask if you are that concerned.'

'I'm not. For heaven's sake sit down.'

'If I do, will you please give me your undivided attention?' She smiled and faced him. 'That's better. I began to feel that I was the waiter.'

'Sorry, Paul.' Suddenly contrite, she put a hand over his on the table. He had gone to a lot of trouble for her tonight and the price of the meal must have stung him heavily. 'I'm all ears,' she said. 'Tell me about your next project.'

Usually this was enough to send him off into details about place names, family trees and family likenesses until she felt like going off to sleep or made mental notes of shopping lists and when her laundry was due back from the cleaners, but he seized her hand and leaned forward. 'About time, too. When do I move in with you, Kit? I've asked you before and it's time you stopped messing about and made it a firm arrangement.'

'I told you that I like living alone, Paul. I can't have you there. There just isn't room for two, unless we were living together in every sense of the word.'

'So?'

'No, Paul. Let me make this clear. I have never lived with a man and I have no intention of doing so.'

'Not even if I asked you to marry me?' She stared. 'Don't look so surprised. I couldn't ask you until I was on an upturn.' His eyes gleamed. 'You know the boat just down the creek? Been empty during the winter but they are scraping and painting now ready for hire or sale. It's quite big and there would be enough room for my books and files. We could put a deposit on it and get married next month.'

'I can't.'

If he had asked her to live with him and shrugged as he did when he couldn't get his own way, the evening would have gone on as had so many others, with the subject dropped until next time, but this was so different. He looked more confident, more determined and she felt as if she was being driven up into a cul-de-sac that narrowed her way of escape and all her options.

'You must.' The voice was cool and unlike his

usual warm drawl. 'I need you, Kitty, and I want you badly. You can go on working. You'd have to for a while, but we could get settled in quite soon before I start another book.'

She took her hand away and sipped more wine. Chairs scraped back and she glanced up towards the table where Carol Gaynor was sitting. The couple came towards Kitty and Carol smiled. 'Sister Martin! How very pleasant.' Her gaze flickered past Kitty to Paul who sat back, annoyed by the interruption. 'I hope you enjoy your evening. This is quite good, isn't it?'

'It's the first time I've been here,' said Kitty.

'How are the people at Osborne?' Carol smiled. 'I'm just back from America and I haven't had a chance to visit. Alex asked me to look in to see them all. Is Rory Oliver still there? And Bruce Mycroft?'

'Captain Oliver has gone home to Devon. Bruce has his assessment soon and will pass easily, and Basil Sinclair is miraculously better.'

'Bruce went sailing with you. Well done.' She smiled, and Kitty found it impossible to think she was either shallow or unfeeling. Carol looked up at her escort. 'He went sailing with you, too, didn't he?'

'Yes, Blanche brought him over and he's really keen.'

'There's a lot of catching up to do after only ten days away.' She looked up at the man with her and her eyes held the tender, misty expression that

Kitty had seen her give to Alex Roscoe, the kind of expression she had imagined would be for him alone. Carol put a small hand on his arm. 'Patrick is so good to me. He met me off the plane and brought me here this evening for a chat before I see Alex and Basil again.'

'You expect to see them soon?'

'Of course. Didn't Alex tell you?'

'He hasn't been on duty for days.'

'He hasn't rung you?'

'Once, to ask about his mail.' And she wanted to say that the letter that left his voice sombre and sad was the one she had sent. 'Oh, yes, he also rang to break a dinner date with me and Blanche.'

'So you know! And you did know that he is coming to stay with Basil when he comes to Patrick?' She laughed. 'What a re-union it will be.'

'Sounds fun,' said Kitty.

'You must come over for dinner.' She laughed. 'I know I am not the hostess, but I can speak for Patrick and his wife.' He smiled and nodded, and Kitty felt her own smile frozen on her face.

'Did you enjoy your transatlantic trip?' she said. Anything to take the conversation away from the fact that Alex didn't care enough about her to be in touch when he was away but coming back to East Cowes.

'Not really, but I had to go. It was all arranged so beautifully that I couldn't back out even when I would rather have stayed here.' She smiled, gently.

'Let's say it was an experience I wanted but I shall never go there again.' She sighed. 'It all had a kind of excitement but I was so glad to see your face at the airport, Patrick.'

Kitty picked up her handbag as if preparing to leave.

'We haven't had coffee yet and we have things to discuss, Kitty,' said Paul in a loud voice.

'I'm sorry I disturbed you,' said Carol. She was once more formal and very polite. 'Please drop in to see us all. Basil in particular will be bored as he can't do a lot, I assume?' She went away, with Patrick holding her elbow as if he expected her to break in two.

Kitty accepted coffee and added sugar that she seldom had. Carol Gaynor must be some kind of siren, making men fall in love with her sweet expression, the husky voice, the spun-gold hair and the wistful eyes. First Alex Roscoe, who she kissed and called darling, and then left him for a holiday on some foreign beach when another man who was a dear friend fought for mobility and longed for her hand in his, and now Patrick, a married man who looked at her in the same way, as if she should be spoiled, made a cherished doll and indulged in anything she wanted.

'She's a bit of all right,' said Paul, coarsely.

'Men do find her attractive,' said Kitty.

'I can imagine, but not my type. She would never mend my socks and do my filing.'

'Nor would I. The difference being that she

doesn't have to refuse to do it. No man would expect her to do such menial jobs.'

Strange, she thought. I think she might be a nurse, too, but her life will be miles away from my situation and she will have everything she desires; clothes, homes and men to love her. She can have everything if I can have Alex Roscoe. But it was no use. Carol would have it all in one delightful, overpowering golden gift. If she had Alex, she would have everything.

'Now where were we?' said Paul. 'I was about to suggest that you come with me to sign on the dotted line for the houseboat.'

'Don't you ever listen, Paul? I said NO! That means No, *non*, *nein*, or whatever it is in all languages.' She laughed. 'Don't be silly, Paul. I want to see the world before I settle down. I might travel and see the States. I could work in a wealthy clinic, looking for a millionaire. I'll come back with a sun tan that will dazzle even the jet set of Cowes Week.'

'Your friend isn't very tanned if she's come back from some coral beach or whatever.' He laughed. 'Obviously not sunny California or Florida.'

'She did look pale.' Kitty wondered what the name of the place was that was mentioned in the letter. Any beach mentioned hinted of hot sun and cool long drinks by white sands, with bikini-clad bodies roasting happily.

'Perhaps she had a dose of Montezuma's revenge or whatever they call the runs in her part of the world.'

'She looked tired rather than ill.' Kitty finished her coffee. 'Let's go, shall we? I have to be up early and I haven't sorted out my laundry yet.'

'When are you off duty tomorrow? At least look at the houseboat. It's really great, Kitty.'

'When can I see it? I am not going to leave my own but I have a passion for seeing other people's wallpaper. I'm off tomorrow afternoon.'

'That's awkward.'

'You said any time.'

'In fact, I'm coming over to Osborne tomorrow afternoon. The Royal apartments are still closed to the public, but I have an appointment with the Controller who is very helpful. I can work in the study for two hours and take a few notes. It should be quite a source of names and families among the people who worked there and had connections with the Royal family.'

'So, I'll wave to you as I leave,' she said, lightly. 'I shall go back home to paint another door and to repair the damage you caused to my efforts.'

'Why not stick around? You enjoy the House, don't you?'

'You mean, will I stay and take notes for you! I'm not that keen, Paul.'

It was there again. One minute she thought of him as a thoroughly pleasant companion who could, in the course of time become more, and then there crept in a sneaking feeling that she was being used. So many times she had washed clothes that he just happened to have with him after the launderette was shut, she had cooked meals to which he homed in as if given a signal and he borrowed holdalls and blankets for working trips when he camped in barns and in another borrowed tent.

'I'll see you soon,' was all that she would promise, and when she was caught up in the routine next morning, she forgot Paul and his pressing desire to take her over. The contrast between the time when there were few people at Osborne and today was very marked. A few people left by the morning ferry and twelve fresh faces appeared soon after eleven, ready to take their places in the beautiful house. So much had to be arranged that it was a shock to be told that it was lunchtime and that her off duty had begun.

'By the way, Sister. There was a telephone call for you when you were out in the grounds showing someone where they could sit if the weather is fine. Nobody could find you and I saw you only when he had rung off.' The secretary was apologetic. 'He seemed annoyed and I'm sorry if it's put you to any inconvenience.'

'Did he leave a message?' Kitty wasn't very concerned. Paul never gave up. He might think that if he caught her before she left, she would reconsider and spend the sunny afternoon cooped up with him and his books.

'No, he wouldn't say who was calling.' The girl blushed. 'Oh, dear, I'm not doing very well. There was a note, too. It was handed in about an hour ago.'

Kitty took the small envelope and wondered who had bothered to send a note. Paul wouldn't do so and in any case, his notes were usually torn from notebooks or on the backs of envelopes. This was good notepaper and the card inside was thick and expensive.

'Come to dinner after duty tonight,' said the cryptic message. 'May we use your brains to prepare for Basil?' It was signed by Blanche and the address and a scribbled map was on the reverse side of the card.

She stared at the card. They needed her help, so they just sent for her as if she was in their employ. No, that wasn't quite fair. Blanche really did like her and if she hadn't been so involved with Bruce, would have spent a lot of time with her.

'Not bad news, I hope?'

'No,' Kitty forced a smile. 'Just an invitation, but it reminded me of something.' She picked up her bag. 'I shall be back this evening but I shall be out of the building until six. I am not going straight home after duty tonight, so if anyone enquires, would you say I can't meet anyone at my home until tomorrow?' That would settle Paul for another day, she thought. It also made up her own mind. If she was to go out with Blanche and the others, she must go back to the houseboat for suitable clothes and makeup to save time after duty.

The sun was warmer than at any time during the past few weeks and it could mean a spell of really good weather that might last. Boat owners would be rowing out to neglected sailing dinghies and cabin cruisers after the winter, wishing they had done more work at the end of the sailiing year and were not faced with the drab paint and repairs that had seemed so unimportant when rain lashed the river and the mud of the Creek caked sea boots and cold fingers dropped stiff paint brushes. She parked by the houseboat and walked down to the muddy shore where her own dinghy was tied up. She smiled, ruefully. I'm no example, she thought. The paint was dingy and when she looked in the sail locker, a musty smell met her. She changed into old jeans and a thick sweater and rubber boots. The breeze was drying and when she hauled the sails out to spread on the deck and over the boom, the thought of the sea and the summer to come made her smile.

A man strolled by and stopped to watch her. 'Hello, Sister,' he said. 'Want any help?' He grinned. 'I'm Sam's brother. You know our Sam down on the ferry? He said you wanted a few jobs done and I can spare a bit of time.'

'I can't afford to pay someone to paint the house-boat. I might want this one cleaned up a bit but I haven't assessed the damage yet. I've a feeling that the helm isn't right. Can you do boats?'

'Do anything, Sister. Let's have a look.' He climbed down the bank and stepped on board the sailing dinghy, leaving muddy marks all over the deck. 'I like boats,' he said, but watched her heave up another sail without offering help.

'I'll let you know,' she said. 'I think I'll take her out first and see how she does.'

'I could come.'

'No, Pete. Not now.' She had sampled some of Sam's work and if his lack of finish and skill ran in the family, she could bear not to have Pete with her in his smelly jersey.

'You'll want that fixed.' He pulled off the sliding hatch cover that showed a split down the middle. 'Get a bit of a breeze up and you'll ship water.'

She hesitated. 'Very well. Take it away and mend it. But I have to know what you charge, as I haven't money to burn.'

'I'll see you all right, Sister.' His smile was expansive. 'Don't you worry.'

'I'm not worrying. That's why I want a firm price now, Pete, or you can forget it.' His smile faded slightly. 'Come on, Pete. Stop wasting my time.'

'Sam said there were no flies on you, Sister.' He named a price that was less than Kitty had expected. She pretended to consider it carefully and then nodded.

'All right, and we'll see how you do,' she said.

He loaded the wood on to the side car of his motor-cycle and drove off in a cloud of blue smoke. Sam's expertise with engines obviously didn't include servicing the family vehicles.

She hoisted a storm jib although the breeze was very light. Better be careful the first time and not go far. She cast off and tried the engine. Once or twice it had been started during the winter to make sure it was working, and this time, it spluttered as if water had got in the oil, but it soon cleared and the boat chugged listlessly out into mid stream.

She glanced at the banks and saw that it was coming up for full tide. Just enough left to bring her back to the houseboat after half an hour afloat. The sail flapped and she was glad that the engine was working. Meadows of lush spring grass fell astern and cows were pulling at the spring bite. It was wonderful to be free and to have the wind in her hair. She stood by the helm and frowned. It was very much out of true and she decided to turn back. In the distance, she saw another boat, with sleek lines and immaculate paintwork. It reminded her of the yacht she had seen through the telescope, but this was no time to stay and make polite conversation even if it was Patrick's boat. The tide was good and took her back quickly. She shaded her eyes to see who was on board the other vessel, which now seemed to be anchored. Two men were on deck and her heart beat faster. The man standing by the boom looked dark and had wide shoulders.

Crossly, she concentrated on getting back to base. I imagine I see him everywhere, she thought. So why not here? It was possible. Nobody at the home had mentioned that he would be back soon, but he might be spending some leave with the friends at East Cowes to be ready to welcome Carol back again to her circle of admiring slaves. She tied up the boat and packed away the freshened sails. If

Pete was any good as a carpenter, he might have a go at the helm. She didn't feel like risking the boat out in the main stream before it was fixed.

CHAPTER SIX

WALKING from her car over the gravel path made Kitty wish that she had worn less delicate shoes, but as soon as she rang the bell of the L-shaped bungalow and saw how her hostess was dressed, she was glad that she had made the effort to look as good as possible.

'I'm Debbie, Patrick's wife. I've been dying to meet you, Kitty.' The pretty girl was almost as blonde as Carol Gaynor and there was a family resemblance, which accounted for her spending so much time with them.

'It was nice of you to invite me,' said Kitty. 'I'm sure you must have quite enough to do without entertaining strangers.'

'Strangers? I feel that we know you already. Come in and meet the others.' She looked at Kitty with amused appraisal. 'I love that skirt. Liberty, isn't it?'

Kitty nodded. The rich shades of deep red and brown with echoes of green and ochre that made up the abstract print of the fine wool circular skirt merged with the soft green of her sweater and the shiny brown shoes. A heavy brooch of mixed semi-precious stones glowed in dull beauty, catching the ends of the three-cornered shawl that matched the skirt, and antique ear-rings peeped fleetingly through the thick shiny brown hair.

They went into the sitting room where a wide picture window looked out on to the sea, seen through a mist of weeping willow on one side and flanked by flowering shrubs, making a perfect frame for the blue water and the boats that sailed across the vista. Kitty found herself drawn to the window, to look out rather than to examine the room. 'It's beautiful,' she said. 'From the road, I had no idea that the house was so near the beach.' She saw the yacht moored to the slender jetty and the fibreglass tender, beached ready to take passengers out to the boat. The boat was in darkness and one lone sea bird sat high on the masthead as if guarding it for the night.

'Come and have a drink before we eat. Carol will be here soon with Patrick and we can eat and talk.' She poured sherry into fine crystal and they sat by the window as the light left the bay. Kitty wondered if her hostess was so sure of her husband's fidelity that she could afford to let him go away for hours at a time with the lovely blonde woman who seemed to have a mesmeric effect on men.

As if reading something of her thoughts, Debbie said, 'Carol is my cousin, you know. She is such a part of our life that I hate it when we don't see her often enough.' She seemed to brood. 'We naturally want to do everything for her now that she is quite alone in the world except for us, and I hope that she will come back to us when she can spare the time.'

'She has already been away. I'm sure that Commander Roscoe missed her very much,' Kitty said.

It was an effort to keep calm. Everyone made excuses for the girl, as if she could do as she liked and still be spoiled by an adoring set of relatives and the men who loved her. Ten days away when Basil was having a crucial operation which might decide his future and his plans for the rest of his life—surely that was a cruel neglect of a friend when he needed all the encouragement and affection she had to give. But had she much love to offer anyone but Carol Gaynor? The soft glances she gave to Alex Roscoe and Basil Sinclair were the same as those she cast towards Patrick, with all the wiles of a kitten wanting attention.

'Yes, it was a pity she had to go away so abruptly, but she had no choice with everyone being so kind. It was all arranged so she couldn't refuse to go. In a way, she looked on it as a duty.'

Kitty turned away, unable to hide her irritation. Some duty! A duty to whom? The airline for accepting her booking for a luxury holiday in the sun? Then she recalled what Paul had said, and he was right. Carol had come back looking pale as if she had been to the North Pole instead of a sunny beach in America.

'Here they are.' Debbie went to the door and called to Patrick and soon the room seemed filled with people. Carol was elegant in pale grey velvet that sat in a svelte line over slim hips and Blanche bubbled with good humour, her dress a flame of gold and amber that set off her dark colouring superbly. Bruce Mycroft came in almost shyly. He kissed Kitty on the cheek.

'I didn't think they let residents out at night,' she teased.

'You can't rule me now, Sister Martin.' He laughed. 'Seriously, Kitty, I'm delighted to see you here. It's time you met the rest of this marvellous crowd.' He accepted his drink with a smile at Blanche. Kitty saw the exchanged smiles in which there lurked a promise and an understanding. 'Shall we tell her, Blanche?'

'She knows. These nurses read the minds of everyone.' She laughed. 'Well, almost everyone. Alex finds you a little obtuse at times, but then, he would.'

'What do you mean?'

'You know how he is. He locks up his own reactions to circumstances and people and then grumbles that he is misunderstood.'

'I suppose he is the strong silent type,' said Kitty, trying to smile.

'Alex? You have to be joking. I think that having suffered quite a lot after the Falklands, he now knows more about the feelings of people like Basil who have had to come back time and time again for more surgery. Alex must be very glad that he has nothing more to face and can forget his back as soon as the scars fade.'

Kitty wondered if Blanche had been told that the puckered scars on the surgeon's back would just fade and be invisible in time. Surely she must know that they needed to be tidied up if they were to go away, with some of the skin taken and the new sutures inserted under the edges so that no stitch holes were evident? She could imagine Alex brushing aside any comment and wearing covering shirts for the rest of his life.

Blance looked towards the door. 'Oh, here they are, better late than never,' she said cheerfully, and went to greet Basil and Alex who stood in the doorway.

Basil stared past everyone and his eyes saw only Carol. It was so obvious that he adored her that Kitty felt quite sick. Carol was smiling and she went to him and held his arm as he walked slowly to a high-backed chair. He was thin and paler than Kitty remembered him but his eyes were not febrile as they had been the night he was taken to the Naval hospital in a hurry. He walked well but with caution and seemed very happy.

She was so fascinated by his reaction to Carol that she stared and when Alex spoke to her, she looked up as if seeing him for the first time. In one way she was, as he no longer wore the loose-fitting track suit in which he seemed to live. She caught her breath. His tight-fitting black trousers outlined every line of his virile body and the blue silk shirt with the high neckline, made his eyes look very blue. Gone were the grey glints that hardened his hawklike gaze and his hair shone and curled round his ears as if caressing them.

He came towards her and she knew that she had worn just the right clothes. If only he could love her and not just find her attractive. He took her hands in his and she blushed under the intent inspection.

'Have I a smut on my nose?' she said, the tension becoming unbearable.

'Yes,' he said, and kissed the tip of her nose. She drew away, knowing that her pulse was rising. The others all seemed engrossed in cosy twosomes and they were alone by the wide window. He seemed to recover, as if he had been tempted into an action that was not permitted. 'You look very delectable,' he said, formally, and she knew that his kiss was no more than the continental greeting. He followed the others into the dining room with Kitty by his side and she found that Debbie had put them together at table.

It was easy to see now why she had been invited. If Carol was making a play for Basil, then Alex would be embarrassingly alone, forced to be in the same room as the woman he loved and having to watch her with another man. And the two heads were almost touching as Carol placed a cushion at Basil's back and gazed fondly down at him. I am not needed to advise about beds and chairs and comfort for a man who needs nothing but one stick when he walks far and has a nurse to hover over him, with no sign that he was angry because she had neglected him, Kitty thought. The avocado and crab, the roast pheasant and delicious sorbets could have been beans on toast and icecream as far as Kitty was concerned. She ate and drank and listened to the bright conversation. Everyone seemed happy except her and as she glanced at Alex, he didn't seem very happy either. Her heart ached for him. Her own love for him was . . . her own, and there was no other person who knew about it, but all these people must know how he felt about Carol.

They discussed Osborne and Cowes Week, and Patrick asked Kitty if she had done any racing.

'Not really,' she said. 'I was brought up with old boats that did very little but drift about the river. My family never had a boat suitable for racing, as my father wasn't a competitive type. I raced with local clubs in the junior sections and I now have a wreck of a boat tied up by my houseboat, but I can't say I'm a member of the sailing fraternity. I'm just a fairweather sailor who likes to be with boats and enjoys the water.'

'We'll have to change all that, eh, Alex? Alex loves sailing. Keener than me, really.'

Blanche was listening. 'I used to tease him and say that you could recognise a sailor on leave at the seaside because he would be the first to hire a boat. Even on the Serpentine in London, there are ratings in skiffs on any fine day in summer. All fresh from their boats. You'd think they'd have had enough of the sea after weeks on board.' She turned to Carol as everyone sat back and sipped the last of the wine and nibbled cheese. 'Do you think you can take another stint at sea?' she asked, bluntly.

'I'll have to go if I'm sent.' She smiled. 'But I don't want to think about that now.' She looked down at her plate, and Kitty caught a glimpse of something like fear in her eyes.

Patrick raised his glass. 'This is something of a farewell party for Carol who has to report back soon. To you, Carol dear, and a good life.'

She really did have tears in her eyes now. 'You promised to let it ride, Pat.' She glanced down at Basil who reached over and took her hand.

'Sorry, dear,' said Patrick, 'but it had to be said. We all love you and want you back to normal. Don't stay away too long.'

'Thank you.' She smiled and seemed to brace herself. 'There are things I can't talk about even now, but I am getting better.' Basil murmured something and she looked at him, tenderly. 'One day I'll write it all down, but not now,' she said.

'Coffee in the sittingroom,' said Debbie, firmly.

Kitty could no longer contain her curiosity. 'You are in the Naval Nursing Service, Carol?'

'Didn't you know? I thought Alex told you.' She gave him an exasperated and amused glance. 'Really, Alex!' He smiled and said nothing. 'I'm sorry, Kitty. I must need my head examined. If you didn't know, then all our talk must have been terribly confusing. I have to go back on duty tomorrow at the base hospital. I've had very generous leave and been on light duties ever since I was at sea, and now I have to plan where I am to make a permanent base.'

'You have Debbie and Pat.' Kitty looked across at Basil. 'And Basil.'

'Yes, I have Basil.' Carol let out a long sigh and, for the first time, Kitty noticed faint lines round her mouth.

Debbie was switching on lights with shaded bowls that threw gentle pools of light at strategic points in the sitting room. Kitty followed to help draw the curtains over the now dark windows, and as she pulled on a silk cord, she saw a solitary boat far out on the Solent with its navigation lights the only sign of life. I shall never be anything but solitary in an alien world unless I put Alex from my mind and take up with Paul, she thought. Pat brought her some coffee and Alex once more sat near to her. Poor man, she thought. Carol appears to have settled for Basil and makes no secret of that fact, so he needs me at least for tonight to fill a gap and to make up numbers at Debbie's table.

'You are off duty tomorrow, I believe?' said Alex. He handed her some Drambuie. 'Any plans?'

'I left a message with an odd-job man to fetch the rudder and helm from my boat and mend them. He rang to say he had finished another job I gave him to do, so I thought he might be able to put the rudder in a vice to trim it before I decide to buy another. It didn't look very hopeful when I took it out for a trial.'

'Was that you out there today?' Pat looked interested. 'We thought it was you, but you hared off before we could make contact. I said at the time that you were making a rather weird course, but Alex said that he wasn't surprised.' He laughed and she had the impression that the men were amused at her expense.

'I was being wary. I tested the boat before high tide so that I knew I could drift back to the moorings if all failed on board. The engine was fine but the steering was futile.'

'You must try our boat sometime. We all sail and we must arrange a picnic lunch party.'

'Why not go to France? We could make it a weekend trip if you don't mind sharing a cabin,' said Debbie.

'That would be lovely,' said Kitty, politely.

All these plans, but she knew that they would come to nothing. Alex would go back on active duties and Bruce would go away on leave, Carol back to the hospital and the others busy with their normal lives. And Kitty Martin would do what?

'And when you have finished with your boat?' Kitty stared at Alex. 'You have a day off, remember?' She nodded. 'I wonder if you could do me a favour?'

'Of course.'

'My car is being used tomorrow. It's big and comfortable and I told Blanche to use it to take Bruce to the West Wight, but now I find that I have business in Cowes and Newport. Could you bear to drive me?'

Blanche came and leaned over her chair. 'You

are an angel, Kitty. This will be my last day with Bruce for some time. I have to go to Hong Kong the day after tomorrow and he has to go away, too.'

Alex went for more coffee. 'I hope you have a wonderful day,' said Kitty.

'You do like Alex, don't you?' For a moment, Blanche looked doubtful.

'He's a fine man,' said Kitty. 'I'll be pleased to help.' She smiled. 'You're just right for Bruce.'

'I know,' said Blanche, complacently. 'It takes some men time to know what's best for them, and I am best for Bruce.' She looked up with a wicked smile as Alex handed her a cup and saucer.

'You scheme too much,' he said. 'It doesn't always work.'

His smile was forced, and Blanche looked puzzled.

'I thought I did rather well on the whole.' She laughed. 'One thing I must do, Kitty. I must have your address so that I can send you an invitation to our wedding.' She looked radiant. 'We can't make a date yet but it will be soon.'

'You'll have to make it for two, Blanche. I think that Kitty has been holding out on you. Carol was telling me that she saw you in the new roadhouse with a boy friend. It might be tactful to find out if he should be asked, too.' He picked up his cup and went across to talk to Debbie.

'Oh, dear,' said Blanche.

'Don't worry. Paul is a friend I've known for a

long time, but we don't live in each other's pockets.'

'I'm glad. He doesn't object to you nursing a lot of rather attractive males?'

'Why should he? It's my job. He's an historian and writes books, so we don't see a lot of each other.'

'Are you in love with him, Kitty.'

'I'm very fond of him,' she said. 'He has asked me to marry him.'

Blanche looked shocked. 'You can't do that. You don't love him enough to marry him.'

'We get on fine,' said Kitty and was glad when Patrick came to ask if she wanted any more to drink. 'No,' she said. 'I must get back to my tacky boat. It would be lovely if the paint has dried.' She found her car keys and saw that Alex waited by the door, wearing a jacket over his shirt. 'There's no need,' she said.

'We haven't made arrangements for tomorrow.' He followed her out when she had said her farewells and shone a torch down on the uneven driveway. 'It's tricky along here,' he said, and tucked her hand under his arm.

The contact was almost frightening. He had been close to her during dinner with only fleeting touches of hand against sleeve, or shoulder against his, which made her aware of him as a man of intense sexuality, a pleasantly dangerous feeling that made her forget what she was eating and what other people were saying, but this was just the two of them in a dark place, with the fragrance of the green spring about them and the sound of a distant ship's siren out in the Roads. It had been a sound that she had loved since childhood, and still filled her with the mystery of a voice calling across the lonely sea. She shivered and he put an arm round her shoulders, drawing her close and turning to watch the join of dark sea with brighter sky.

He put the torch down on a low wall and held her close. His face in the starlight was carved out of stone and his eyes told her nothing but burned with a deep desire that could have been for the love he had lost, or could have been the sudden need for the soft lips and body of any pretty girl. He bent to kiss her and she knew that 'this was the hour of knowing'.

Her lips were soft as the primroses on a green bank and his hands found her waist and she was pressed against the firm thighs that wanted her so badly. She sensed that all the agony of celibacy was fighting his reserve and his sense of right and she knew with black certainty that she was only the instrument of release. He had watched the woman he wanted give her love and troth to another man, and his own sister was to be married soon. He would be alone with just fly-by-night affairs to satisfy his deep need for love and sex and fulfilment.

He kissed her again and again with sorrow in his eyes, and she responded in shared sorrow. How could she let this happen? She arched her back away from his kisses but he found the curve of her throat where it blossomed into the fullness of her breast. She pushed him away and stood with her hair in disorder and her lips trembling.

'You are the loveliest girl I have ever known,' he whispered. 'Stay with me, Kitty.'

'No, I have to go.' She was sure that if she stayed for another minute, all her defences would crumble and she would be lost for ever. 'Alex, you have to let me go.' It was a cry of agony, of pleading, to help her find the strength to resist him, but as his hands fell to his sides, she knew that he was remembering Paul. He couldn't have the woman he loved and now he had to give back the woman he desired to a faceless man who had held her hand in a restaurant.

'I'm sorry,' he said. 'You seemed . . . content to be with me, and this evening you were one of the family. I had no right to force you.'

'I understand, Alex.' She reached up and kissed his cheek. 'I'm sorry too.'

'Promise me that you will never go to a man who can't make you completely happy.'

'Do we ever get complete happiness?' she said.

'Either find it perfect, or do without,' he said. 'You weren't built for compromise.'

'And you, Alex?'

'I have yet to find out if my life can ever be complete,' he said. He picked up the torch and took her to the car.

She never could remember the silent drive home. His face seemed to hover above the rear-view mirror as if he was with her in some phantom of the mind. He did love her, even if only as a substitute for the real passion.

She had come away without making an excuse not to see him the following day but, as it stood, she was due to pick him up at eleven the next morning. She locked the car and shone her torch on to the gangway to her home. It showed a note pinned to the hatch frame, chipping the new paint. It was from Pete, saying that her helm and pivots were OK but the rudder was unfit for repair. 'So I fixed one I got from the yard and I think will do you fine. The screws are a bit off, but I tightened them. She'll do a treat.'

She changed her shoes and went down to look at the boat, but the mud had tipped her sideways and she couldn't see the rudder. Tomorrow, she thought. Tomorrow, I'll do my duty and take Alex on his visits and in the evening, I can try her out before high tide. She locked her door and saw that the mended hatch cover was neatly done. If he did all his work as efficiently, she had no need to worry about the rudder.

She went to bed feeling as if she had watched a sad film or been told that someone had died. I have to make up my mind that I shall never have Alex, even as a lover, she told herself. It might even be better if she addressed him as Commander once they were working back at the Home.

The smell of paint was fading and she thanked modern air fresheners for their effectiveness. It was less draughty and more secure if she could shut some of the windows. She prepared for bed and was brushing her hair when the telephone rang. She started, her heart pounding. The telephone link was a mixed blessing that took a little time to take in her stride. It had been fixed only a month earlier and it gave her a shock each time it rang.

'Katharine Martin,' she said.

'Alex Roscoe,' he said, and cleared his throat. 'You left in rather a hurry. Two things. Blanche wanted your address and although I have this number, I couldn't tell her where you live.' She told him the details and described the situation of her houseboat. 'And if she did happen to call sometime, she wouldn't be intruding?'

'Of course not.' She was surprised. Blanche was such an easy person once the first introductions were over. 'She's welcome any time I'm here. I seldom have people on the boat.' She paused. He had said two things. 'I hope that Basil wasn't too tired,' she said, to break the silence.

'He went to bed in a state of euphoria. Carol has finally said she'll marry him.'

'And you are glad?'

'He needs her. He needs the love of a wife and the care of a nurse for a while, just until one scar has been grafted.'

'And you don't need a nurse, but if you did, there would be plenty willing to care for you.' She tried to sound casual. If he wanted her to think that he had no lasting interest in Carol, it might be better so.

'You make it sound very commercial.'

'Most services are unless you have a wife who will give up everything to look after you. Basil is fortunate; or will be when she does give up her work for him, if she can do that. So she chose him.'

'You sound angry. Why don't you like Carol?'

'I do like her.' She tugged at her hair with the brush, making the scalp tingle as she pulled at the roots. 'And it's not my business what she does.'

But she couldn't hide the tremor in her voice. He had telephoned because he had to talk to someone sympathetic, who knew Carol and knew that his love for her was hopeless. If she could have reached out to smooth back the dark hair and to kiss away his sadness, she could ease her own terrible longing and the sense of injury she felt for him because Carol was so fickle.

'I get the impression that you think Carol should be in love with me.' Anger was growing between them. 'I've known for some time that Basil would marry her as soon as she was settled in her mind.'

'And until then, she could flirt with every man in sight, and make them believe that she loved them.'

'Carol is a very dear person and I do love her. Many people love her in many ways. I thought it was time to clear up a few woolly things you think about her. I love Carol. Of course I love her—she has deserved the love and respect of everyone she meets! What you don't know is that she was married to a great friend of mine in the Navy.'

Kitty felt cold. Poor man, this was something more. He had been in love with a married woman with enough experience of men to be able to twist him round her delicate finger and make him run to her whenever she needed a spare partner. No wonder his stifled desire had risen in a sudden passion when they were alone together in the scented night. To have any woman close to him who was desirable must be an agony of frustration after the self-control he must impose when he was with Carol.

'I didn't know she was married.'

'And you didn't know she was a widow?'

'Oh, *no*!' She shrank back as if from a blow and sat heavily on a chair.

His voice was gentle. 'I thought not. There is more that you should know. I should have made sure that you knew, but I thought Blanche would have told you.'

'Blanche is like you, she doesn't talk about her friends.'

'I should have told you,' he insisted. 'Carol was in the Southern Ocean with us, as a nurse. Her husband was there too, and went down with his ship.'

'Oh, no. *No*!' Her whisper held everything of her shame. 'She was working in the hospital ship when he . . . oh, no.'

'You are crying! Kitty, are you still there?'

'Yes, I am crying. Poor Carol.'

'She has wept all her tears, at least in public. She did that some time ago and then finally washed her grief away on Blue Beach and San Carlos Water.'

'Blue Beach?' She remembered the name.

'Didn't you know? That's the beach where troops landed and died. The cemetery at San Carlos is near and she went this year with relatives of the dead for a memorial service.' He could hear the stifled sobs. 'Kitty, no woman wants a man who is maimed, does she? He died and she can remember him as he was.'

'That explains so much,' she said. And it also explained why she had to go away when Basil, with whom she was falling in love, was hovering on the brink of disaster.

'She went away to make up her mind. She told me that whatever happened to Basil, she would care for him and love him, but she had to say goodbye to her ghosts first.' He spoke briskly. 'So, no tears for Carol. She is tougher than you think. She is picking up the threads and is going to live life to the full again.'

'They had no children?'

'No, they had been married for only a year. Hardly time to get to know each other. I introduced them and it was a very quick courtship and marriage. They had so little time together and I wondered if she had married the right man.' He sighed. 'I'm sure she has chosen the one she really loves this time, and she has lots of very loyal friends.'

'And you will be there if she needs you.'

'Of course.' He laughed, lightly. 'But not to-morrow. You are taking me out and then I shall buy you lunch. We never did have that dinner party we arranged.'

'No, we couldn't make it.'

'Did I disturb you tonight?'

'No,' she lied. When had she ever heard his voice and remained calm? When could she forget that dark head and those shattering blue-grey eyes?

'I can imagine you there,' he said. 'Let me think . . . You are ready for bed?'

'I was brushing my hair when the phone rang.'

'That rather lovely but tortured hair that goes neatly into severe rolls just where Sister Martin wants it?'

'Not now. It's loose.'

'Of course it is, if you are brushing it. And are you warm enough sitting there in something as flimsy as a whisper?' She blushed and drew the kimono closer over her breasts.

'I wear long flannelette nighties and an old camel-hair dressing gown handed down from my granny,' she said, firmly. She smiled. The dear man was flirting with her to make sure she went to bed without thinking too deeply about Carol and her tragedy, calmer after the emotion he had unleashed when he told her the details.

He had telephoned to rid himself of memories, as Carol had flown to the Southern Ocean to expiate her grief. 'I also put my hair in curlers and smother my face in cold cream.'

'Liar,' he said.

'I seldom lie,' she said.

'I imagine you there with your hair loose, and yet when I close my eyes I see you in uniform, but not at Osborne. I know that I have seen you somewhere, in uniform but in a different setting.'

'I was at Osborne when you were there the first time I worked there.'

'No, not that. You had a cloak and a different cap.'

'Uniforms look alike and most nurses wear cloaks.'

'Where did you train?'

'In Southampton.'

'That wasn't the uniform. I operate in the theatre there quite often, or I did a year or so ago before the Service.'

'I worked in the accident unit at Birmingham.' She heard his low whistle. 'I did six months and came back here for a break.'

'So none of us are as we seem at first glance. Join the club, Kitty. Sleep well. I'll see you tomorrow.'

The line was dead and she was left staring at the silent instrument. What had he meant? She thought back to her time at the accident unit in Birmingham and a pulse in her temple throbbed. It was easy to forget places once she was sheltered by the band of water that was an effective physical and mental barrier between her and the mainland, but all the tensions of that night now came back in a flood. She sank into bed in the dark, the bedclothes high under her chin as if she needed protection again against the cold sleety air that had made her gasp as

she climbed into the ambulance and heard the
sirens of motorway police cars.

'Everyone available on and off duty,' the voice
over the tannoy had said, and she had put her cap
on again and grabbed a thick cardigan to put on
under her cloak. It was dark and the distant lights
did nothing to make it easy. The flash and dazzle
only made the surrounding night darker as the
vehicles found the motorway and the pile-up of
cars.

Ahead were parked cars and lorries not involved
in the crash, their drivers trying to help in the rescue
or sitting dazed and unable to proceed. She picked
her way through broken glass and twisted metal,
unable to think of anything that wasn't to do with
the moment. 'Over here, Nurse.' She went to the
overturned lorry and saw a junior house surgeon
trying to reach a man trapped under his own
crumpled door. A mass of debris added to the
chaos.

'You'll never get in there,' she said. 'I'm smaller
than you.' She glanced at the rugby player's shoulders. 'Give me the syringe as soon as I can reach.'
She began to wriggle through. It seemed an age
before she lay with a piece of something hard and
rough digging into her abdomen, but his outflung
arm was near enough to reach. She felt for his
pulse. 'Still with us,' she called. The man groaned.
'Can you pass the syringe now? He's in a lot of
pain.' She saw the eyes through the dust and gloom.
He looked like a trapped animal caught in a noose

of steel. His lack-lustre eyes held hopelessness and, when she touched his hand, he tried to speak but she smiled and told him the pain would go soon. The jab would help him.

'Just a jab,' she said, briskly. 'They'll get you out in no time.' She felt for his pulse and breathed a sigh of relief. The needle shot home and he didn't wince, but she guessed that he hardly felt it against the crushing pain in his chest. The cab moved slightly and she reached for a box and wedged it to stop any further fall of the heavy cab.

'Come out now.' The voice was low but urgent. 'You can do nothing more. The fire boys are here to raise the cab with winching gear.' But the hand she had grasped now held hers as if it was his only hope and she pressed it firmly to comfort him. If I go now, he'll die, she thought, and knew the slender link was vital to him.

'I'll stay. He needs comfort,' she said. The man tried to smile and then closed his eyes, his hand still firmly in hers.

An hour, two hours and almost complete numbness from the cold later, and two faces appeared in a growing band of light. The firemen half-lifted her frozen body from the cab and ambulance men took the freed man. A violent glare of light made her shut her eyes. 'Damned photographers get everywhere. Not to worry, Nurse. Get you into a warm bed soon.'

And after? She forced herself to think of the two weeks in bed with pneumonia and a jagged tear in her side where the metal had pierced the muscle. Her picture was on the front page of the newspaper and she saw herself as she had been, in the arms of the fireman, but still wearing her uniform cap. 'And I thought I suffered,' she said. 'I know nothing about real suffering even though I have been in this profession for so long.' She closed her eyes and the tears forced a way through, for the man who she had comforted but had died later, for Carol and her grief, and for the man who had seen suffering and been wounded and now faced life on his own because the woman he wanted was once more marrying another man.

Alex Roscoe must have seen the newspaper photograph and tucked away the memory as many faces are tucked away with unimportant sights and sounds. Faces in old films, others in old books cling to the memory, however unimportant.

Tomorrow, he will recall where he saw me and I shall laugh it off as a mere incident. Tomorrow, I shall be the cool woman who drives him to his appointments and he will never know that I have scars on my body, too. Please, send me peace, she prayed, and let my heart keep from breaking for just another day.

CHAPTER SEVEN

'I SAID I'd meet him in the hotel on the front at Cowes,' said Alex Roscoe. He leaned on the car door and smiled at Kitty. 'Are you sure that you can spare your valuable time?'

Kitty blushed. He was regarding her with eyes full of wry humour and the reaction of any healthy male to a good looking woman. She almost wished that she had put her hair up into a roll as she had it on duty, but her natural wish to look good out of uniform had asserted itself and she had dressed as if for a special date. The soft suede jacket of leaf green over a high-necked sweater of cream wool was warm and yet spring like. For driving, she had high leather boots of the same taupe leather as her skirt and a dashing cap dangled from her hand as she stood with him by the car. He opened the back door and swung his briefcase and anorak into the back seat. His movements were relaxed and supple and Kitty had noticed that when he walked to the car he now had no limp and took easy strides with which she would have had difficulty in keeping up, if she had walked with him. There was a subtle difference in his manner, too.

Her heart beat faster. He was so much a part of her dreams that when she was away from him she thought that her dreams exaggerated his masculinity and his animal magnetism, but being with him now, with the morning mist on the sea behind him through the trees, convinced her that her dreams did little justice to the reality of this very attractive man. If I can hide my real feelings today, it will be a miracle, she thought. What a situation! He was convinced that she was engaged to Paul and his sense of fair play might stop him making further attempts to make love to her. If he did kiss her, it would be only in the need for the warmth and passion of another human being. With Carol engaged to Basil, he was free to seduce any girl who fell into his strong hands, and to amuse himself in the part of his heart and mind that treated such liaisons as amusement and nothing more.

'I hope I don't throw you about in the car,' she said. 'I'm getting used to it, but it does kangaroo a bit on hills if I am in low gear.'

'Not to worry,' he said, and smiled. 'I am lucky. My back is fine and my leg feels wonderful after they took out the last splinter that was pressing on the nerve endings near the skin.'

'When was this?'

'When I went to the mainland with Basil, of course.'

'Why of course? Nobody told me. I had no idea you were a patient there.' She went round to her door and sat in the driver's seat. To avoid looking at him, she adjusted the rear-view mirror and the air vents while he took his place beside her.

'I didn't want it all over Osborne,' he said, rather shortly.

'And I would have rushed about telling everyone?' She was hurt that he had been so secretive, not only to her as a friend but as a sister in charge of a unit in which he worked.

'That's not what I meant. I'm sorry; that was a clumsy remark. What I wanted to say was that I didn't want you to know.'

'Why not? I see men before and after operations all the time. One wounded hero is very like another after a while.' Her sense of injury made her sound off-hand.

'I see. And it must be a relief to get away and be with a man who is completely whole and doesn't need you as a nurse. I saw the way you looked at Basil and I couldn't bear that look in your eyes for me, Kitty.'

'But Basil was very badly scarred on his body. I don't cringe away from injury. Bruce knows that and so do the others.'

'And the staff at Birmingham.' He sounded subdued. 'I didn't know about Birmingham when I went to hospital. And it was better this way. I was a patient for only one day and now the scars are neat and I don't mind pretty women looking at them.' He grinned but it was an effort. 'I might make it a fresh approach. Come up and see my scars.' She started the car. 'It makes a change from the etchings.'

'They would be more interesting as they were,' she said. 'And they were not repulsive.'

Smoothly, she gained the main road to the chain ferry and looked straight ahead. She knew that he was searching her face for some reaction.

'How did you know? You never saw them. I took great care that they were never on view at Osborne and in the theatre where I worked.'

'You and Blanche *are* alike,' she said, with maddening humour.

'If you don't explain, I'll put on the hand brake and take you across my knee, Sister Martin.'

'I saw you in the surgeons' room.' She braked as they came to the slope leading to the chain ferry. 'And this is much too public for spanking your driver.' She smiled, sweetly. 'I shall yell sexual harassment and my friend Sam will rescue me.' She waved and Alex saw a large scruffy man in a filthy blue jersey smiling at them. 'Hold tight,' she said. 'The tide is low and the ramp takes a rather nasty angle. This is the first time I've been on the ferry in this car.'

'Let me take over.'

'No, it's my car.' She was beginning to enjoy herself, but she had a feeling that she should make the most of her moment of power as she saw the thunderclouds gathering on his brow. 'It's easier to negotiate than the moped,' she said when they were safely on the ferry.

'That's a relief. I was waiting for that terrible bike to explode under you at any time.'

'I didn't think you recognised me under all my gear.'

'Difficult, but I used my imagination and knew what would be under that helmet and that padded jacket. We found your progress very entertaining.' He was teasing and trying to sound as if he wasn't shaken by the thought that she might have seen his scars.

'How very ungallant to spy on a lady,' she said.

'For a lady who seems fairly emancipated, you are very biased. Just what did you see when you looked through keyholes in the theatre?'

'I didn't look through keyholes. The door to the shower room was open.' She blushed scarlet as soon as she spoke. There could be no doubts now just what she had seen.

'I hope that the sight didn't frighten you.'

'No, why should it? I was surprised to see you there and didn't want to embarrass you so I went round to the other door.'

He glanced down at her pink cheeks. 'You have an unfair advantage over me.'

She gulped. The expression in his eyes almost stripped her, making it quite unnecessary for her to appear before him without clothes. She tried to think of Paul and the houseboat. That would be the sane answer to this insoluble problem. If she didn't say that she was engaged to Paul, she would be so terribly vulnerable the first time she was alone with the Commander.

'Hello, Sister.' Sam's jersey was even more unsavoury at close quarters and she wished that the window wasn't down. 'Pete told me he fixed the rudder.'

'I haven't settled with him, yet. The hatch cover was fine and if the rudder works well, I shall be glad to pay him. I'll see him tomorrow afternoon.'

'They watched you from the Sloop,' said Sam. 'You was going all ways, they said.'

'Thank you for their interest,' she said, drily. 'Nice to know that I might have been rescued if I'd fallen in.'

'You'll be taking it out tonight before full flood, I reckon,' said Sam.

'Right,' said Kitty. 'I think the lorry in front is getting restive. We docked a minute ago, Sam.'

He moved away to let down the ramp. 'You seem very well known,' said Alex.

'I can't take out a moped or a boat in this place without everyone knowing.'

'And you can't eat in a restaurant with a good looking guy without the other half knowing,' said Alex.

'I think the locals have got used to Paul and me by now.' She drove off the ferry and joined the line of cars making for Cowes front. 'I've known him for some time. He's a very interesting man. He's an historian and a writer.' She pulled up at traffic lights. 'Where do you want to go in Cowes?'

Let him think what he liked about Paul. There was no need to lie about their relationship or lack of it. From his face, Kitty drew her own conclusions.

He was piqued as any man might be who was losing grip on a situation when he might have managed to manoeuvre a woman into bed with him.

'In front of the Osborne Hotel, if there's a space,' he said, abruptly. 'Blanche tells me that you are not actually engaged.'

'Not yet,' she said. 'He wants me to look at a houseboat that has more room than mine before I decide.' For some reason Alex looked more cheerful. 'If I sell mine, it will look better painted, so I might as well smarten it up,' she said.

'I hope I'm not stopping you from doing urgent jobs?'

'No, I was only too happy to help out.'

The casual warmth between them was ebbing, and Kitty withdrew into her own thoughts. He had no right to think he could flirt with her when his heart was taken by a woman he could not marry, and if he resented Paul then he was being very unreasonable. 'While you talk business, I want to go to the chandler for some new rope,' she said. 'I want to try out the boat tonight.'

'So you can't be with me all day?' The shutters of politeness were coming down fast. 'What a pity, I was hoping to take you to dinner.'

'I have so little time,' she said. 'I want the boat to be seaworthy before the holiday.'

This formal exchange was chilling, more like an encounter than a getting together . . . a kind of naval engagement when they eyed each other as adversaries. She smiled. 'You should see my ropes.

They are all frayed and I wouldn't trust them in a high wind.'

'I'd like to see it if only to convince myself that it's fit to sail.'

'You must come to tea, some day,' she said. It was her turn to make casual commitments that were never to be taken up.

'I'll hold you to that,' he said.

The car park was nearly empty, and as Kitty opened the door to step out of the car and to walk to the sea wall, another car drew up alongside. It was black and official looking and the man inside looked like someone from the Admiralty. Alex put down his window. 'Clive, you old devil! Nice to see you. I didn't know it would be you.'

'Thought it would save time. I was over here for something else and it's more pleasant than bringing you up to Town.'

Alex opened the door that Kitty had shut. 'Why not talk here. It's private and pleasant.' He looked at Kitty who was beginning to think the visitor would never take his eyes off her. 'This is Miss Martin.'

Kitty tried to look like an official chauffeur but knew that she failed. Clive smiled, eyeing her legs as if he found high boots particularly kinky.

'I don't want you to waste your time,' said Alex, firmly.

'No, of course not. How very great a pleasure to meet you, Miss . . . er . . . Martin.'

'I have business too,' she said, with a sweet smile.

'I'll leave you to talk. How long do you want, Commander?'

'An hour should be enough,' said Clive. 'And then you must allow me to buy you a drink in the hotel, or take you both to lunch.'

'Nice of you,' said Alex, smoothly, 'but we are due in Newport for lunch.'

Kitty turned away and thought she heard Alex say, 'Hands off, you lecherous old devil. She's spoken for.'

She sighed. At least he now knew that she and Paul might have something going. She walked up to the narrow High Street of the small yachting town. Glimpses of the sea between houses and warehouses brought whiffs of seaweed of a pungency that seemed a feature of Cowes. Men in salt-stained blue trousers and Guernseys plodded along the main street, their yellow boots squelching on the tarmac. Sailing clothes were in several shops, without much hope of trade until the easing of the weather brought out wives and girl friends as well as the more weather-resistant males. Kitty was the only woman in the chandler's store.

As always, the smell of oilskins and new rope fascinated her, even though the smell was now muted as more and more synthetic materials were used for ropes and sails. She selected some bright blue nylon rope and two new fenders to replace some lost in a gale during the autumn. The window of a jeweller's shop made her smile. Her grandmother had said so often that these shops existed only to supply gifts to wives who had been left behind while their men went sailing, and for good-bye and thank you gifts for girl friends who filled the bunks of the boats during the sailing. She bought chocolate and boiled sweets, knowing that whenever she wanted something sweet, she was on the houseboat, too tired or too lazy to go to the shops, or the rain was coming down so fast that it seemed ridiculous to get wet just to buy chocolate. Looking ahead to the season, she bought canned foods to stock the boat locker for emergency food if she decided to picnic, and when she went back to the car park she was laden with packages.

'Am I late?' she asked Alex, who was leaning against the stone balustrade that was oddly reminiscent of the one on the terrace at Osborne. Here, he was the only heraldic beast, and it needed no other. His dark hair was ruffled in the breeze and behind him the full billow of a huge blue and orange spinnaker made a splash of pagan colour as a foil for the well-shaped head.

'No, you aren't late.' He smiled. 'Clive sent his apologies. He had to go.'

'But he promised me a drink,' she said.

'You wouldn't like him. He eats little girls for lunch. I'll buy you a drink,' he said.

'I'm driving. Better not now.'

'I was protecting you,' he said, laughing. 'You've no idea what a reputation that man has with women. I have to look after you.'

'I thought I was looking after you today.'

'Surprise, surprise,' he said, softly and she found herself looking into eyes that emanated all the sexuality of a man newly back in circulation and feeling virile.

'Newport now?' she said, shakily.

'If you insist. We ought to get the business over.' He looked at his watch. 'And I did say I would be there this morning.'

'Have you the address?'

'First we call at the hospital close by the old Albany barracks.'

'Not trying to get me to hold a retractor?'

'Who knows?' he laughed. 'I hear that you have many talents that I have yet to discover.' He looked at her more seriously. 'I have two lads there who I tidied up when the balloon went up in the South. They have come back for more treatment and I heard they were here, so I promised to visit.'

She smiled. This was the side of Alex Roscoe that seldom showed and for some reason he was as loath to speak of it as he had been to tell her about his own wounds.

'What happened to them?'

'We found that they had extensive tissue crushed, and apart from crush syndrome, we found that if we cut away injured tissue there was a better chance of avoiding infection and further decomposition. It seemed radical at the time, but when we compared with others treated more conservatively, we saw we were right. We had good results and good drainage where foreign matter was driven in.'

'Are they going to be all right?'

'I want to see them today and to make up my mind if any other treatment is justified. Clive wanted my comments for a summary of successful treatment under emergency conditions. The war had a good side. We learned a lot that can be used in civilian emergencies.'

He moved closer and she almost stalled the engine. 'What makes my sister and me alike?' he said, smoothly. His hand touched her hair where it lay on the soft green of the suede jacket.

'You are getting in the way of the gear lever,' she said, weakly.

'Sweet Kitty, who worried about us all.' His lips brushed her hair.

'Newport,' she said, hastily. 'Is this the entrance to the hospital?' It was safer to keep to the business in hand. A man getting better was often very difficult to keep down, as she knew after nursing three Rugby players in one ward, who were healthy but confined to bed strung up on Balkan Beams. All were married but couldn't resist trying to kiss the nurses, and as for bottom pinching, well every nurse on the ward complained of that at some time or other. She assumed that Alex Roscoe was in a similar mental state. He was in love with Carol, but Kitty with her lovely hair and eyes and figure was close to him. She regretted wearing the light floral scent and the cascade of shining brown hair that flowed down to her shoulders.

Perhaps when Carol was married, he would look

for another woman to marry and there would be no need to chase nursing sisters!

He sat back while she drove into the entrance park of the hospital. It was on the crest of a hill, with the river a silver string below, half hidden by the trees and by a ribbon development of houses along the Cowes Road. The hospital, once used for isolating cases of diphtheria and scarlet fever, now had the air of a busy general hospital and Kitty looked about her with interest. 'I haven't been here for a long time,' she said.

He took her keys and locked the doors. 'We might be some time,' he said. He caught her in his arms and kissed her. She was so surprised that she hung limp in his arms and knew that whatever wounds he had suffered, this man was more than recovered! His body was firm on hers and his arms a trap that bound her closer and closer in mind and body.

'People will think you are saying goodbye to me,' she gasped. 'Hospitals are like railways stations in that way.'

'I know.' He grinned and the eyes were very blue. 'The perfect spot to kiss a pretty girl and everyone approves.'

She looked up and saw two laughing ambulance drivers. To her horror, she recognised one as a regular driver to the other hospital in which she worked occasionally. 'I think it is time you visited your patients,' she said, sternly. 'You realise that you have just ruined my reputation?' She shook her head and let the flowing hair hide her face. 'I shall now have to make a new life in the Outer Hebrides. Everywhere I go here I shall meet someone who has heard idle gossip about me.'

'There is only one defence against gossip.'

'What's that?'

'*Toujours l'attaque!*' He kissed her again and his mouth was warm and as if she had known it forever. She clung to him for a moment of bliss and then moved firmly away.

'Do you fight all your battles like that?'

'I am a man of peace, a healer.' He smiled and then she saw the blue-grey eyes grow serious. 'Let's go. I'd like you to come with me.'

In her bag, Kitty had hastily stuffed some of the chocolate she had bought in Cowes and some of the candies. 'Able-seaman Wright?' asked Alex when the nurse greeted them. A pale-faced boy of about eighteen lay on the bed, reading a girlie magazine which he hastily put under the pillow when he saw Kitty.

'Don't bother, Wright. Miss Martin is a nursing sister. You can't shock her.' He smiled sardonically.

'You don't look it, Miss. Nice of you to see us, sir. Chummy Evans is in the next bed but he's in Physio.' He sat up and Kitty saw the healing scars from a graft on his bare shoulder.

Alex stood by the bed and ran his fingers along one scar. He grunted.

'Doesn't hurt now, sir. That last graft was a

good'un and took a treat. Been a long time. Never thought I'd make it, but, thanks to you, I'm still smiling.'

'That makes two of you. I hear that Evans is better after this lot. When do you go on leave?'

'Next Sunday. The lung is clear and no fluid.'

'You haven't been in hospital ever since the Falklands?' asked Kitty. It seemed appalling.

'No, Miss. I went home in between ops. My cousin in the RAF was there for one time. Didn't get a sniff at the war,' he said, with pride, 'but tries to tell me how it should have been run.'

'I expect that your family were glad to see you home.' She smiled and gave him some of the chocolate.

'Thanks,' he said and laughed. 'My mum had the flags out that day. I felt so lousy I couldn't take it in, but I go back now and enjoy a pint and bore them all rigid about what I did to win the war.'

Alex glanced at the chart hanging on the bed end. 'You've done very well. I had doubts about you when everything was happening at once and then I couldn't get back to check on cases I'd done.'

'Sodding chaos,' said Wright, cheerfully. 'Thought you'd be using toilet rolls soon for dressings.'

Alex turned to Kitty. 'I wouldn't put it quite like that, but it was grim. Supplies were never enough, and we had to improvise. I would never have believed it. When I was a student, I smiled politely when surgeons told us what they used in World War II. But just as well they did tell us. We went back to the Ark! Ever heard of wet sets?' She shook her head. 'We soaked sheets in carbolic solution and spread them over trolleys and tables and put anything we boiled on them to keep sterile until they were used, covered by another sheet, also soaked. We boiled up everything as it came used, and popped in the set, instead of just sterilising for each case as needed. Instruments were there ready in case we met something that an ordinary surgical set didn't fit and it cut down delays. We had to observe local asepsis by the tables as there was dust everywhere else and no time for orderlies to wash walls. I just ignored all the shambles around me.'

'I wish I'd been there,' said Kitty.

'I wish you had been, too.' His eyes were grey with recollection, and once more she was excluded. He laughed. 'It cut us all down to size. Most of us had been using gleaming operating theatres, with twice the equipment we needed and disposable drips and syringes. Most of us would have walked out of any place here with treble the equipment we had to use down there and yet our recovery ratio was very high.'

'I can say that,' said the young sailor. Evans joined him and they shared the sweets. They were like school boys about to be let out for holidays and Kitty hoped desperately that they would not become embittered by hidden scars. She looked at the face beside her and saw in the relaxed mouth that he was deeply involved with these people. The boys could never have known that he was close enough to visit them and yet he had made this special effort to see them. She watched him talking and tried to look at him objectively.

He is at home with these men and the Navy means a lot to him, she thought. Carol would have been perfect for him, knowing about Service life and having shared his experiences. He wants me quite a lot, and Paul has asked me to marry him. There's the difference, if I don't think of my own emotions.

'You look fit, sir,' said Wright. He grinned and looked at Kitty as if to say 'lucky sod to have a pretty nurse all to himself.' He laughed. 'You don't need a nurse now.'

'No, I'm only the driver,' she said, sweetly. 'You have other calls to make, Commander,' she said, and watched the grin die from the boy's face. That's scotched one piece of gossip, she thought, but there would be others if she was seen with Alex too often and certainly if he behaved as outrageously as he had done in the car park.

Would Alex Roscoe go out of his way to compromise her into doing what he so obviously wanted, knowing that she was almost engaged to Paul? His hand was lightly on her arm as they walked back to the car and her mouth felt dry when she thought of the danger of that contact in any secluded spot.

The ward and the corridors were as familiar as

many hospitals in which she had worked. The smell of cleanliness and antiseptics and the calm speed of those who worked there filled her with the pleasure that her work still brought to her. At the entrance, an ambulance stood with a rear door open and a man was being taken into the building on a stretcher. She saw blood on his head and her face paled. It was only on such occasions that she recalled fully the night of the motorway pile-up. To her surprise, Alex held her hand, gently, and when she looked up into his eyes, they were friendly and tender with understanding.

'I recalled where I saw you,' he said. 'It's still with you, isn't it? Just as our lot came back to me when I saw Wright.'

'You can't know. You weren't there,' she said.

'I read the papers.' They reached the car and he opened the door for her and went round to his side. She twisted the keys between her fingers. 'Some pictures stick. Your picture was one.' He looked ahead as if seeing a picture in his mind. 'Once, I remember seeing a picture of a group of children and old people being taken to a German concentration camp. One boy seemed to stand out and his eyes haunted me. He was wearing a stupid cap. I saw the same group in a documentary film and the face was there, just the same, wearing the stupid cap. I almost shouted, Stop, I know that boy! The memory was that sharp. And your face leaped out at me in the same way, as if I would meet you one day.' He looked down at immaculate fingernails. 'It took longer to know you, but women are so unreasonable. They change their clothes.' He grinned and looked up. 'You were wearing uniform and you do look quite different in your Hell's Angels gear, riding that terrible machine.'

'A 50cc moped doesn't make me a Hell's Angel,' said Kitty. She laughed and drove on the road to Newport, where he merely called to leave a letter with a local doctor that could easily have been posted. 'You don't need me,' she said. 'This isn't urgent.'

'I still need tender loving care,' he said, calmly, 'and I like being driven by a beautiful woman.'

'You have enough tender loving care from your friends and your sister.'

'I have hidden scars,' he said, and she bit her lip, knowing the scars of rejection went deep.

'Everyone has them. Where to, Commander?'

'You mean you will sacrifice putting more paint on your boat and have lunch with me?'

'Unless you want me to drop over the wheel weak from hunger.' She tried to sound normal but her heart sang. Why not make the most of just being with him? Why not let this day shine and remain a jewel in the darkness of the future? 'Where would you like to go?' she said.

'You know the place. I want to hear about the Island and about your family. Tell me where they started.'

'They are scattered. Those on my mother's side lived near Carisbrooke but I have no close relatives left. It's still very pretty there and we could get a pub lunch.'

'Fine. I am in your hands.'

Kitty followed the line of old railings that marked the Mall leading to the top end of the town and her mind raced. Why had she suggested Carisbrooke? Yesterday, Paul was at Osborne but his main stamping ground was Carisbrooke and would be until his latest research was complete. He'd muttered something about checking some gravestones in the old churchyard, but with any luck he would not be there now. One of the pubs had a lake behind it, with tumbling water and pretty trees. On reflection, if Paul had lunch out, it would consist of sandwiches eaten on the site and just a beer in one of the other smaller places.

'This used to be good, but I haven't been here for ages,' Kitty said. They sat by the window and ordered Ploughmans with best bitter. Alex watched her butter the crisp French bread and smiled as if the sight pleased him.

'I'd prefer cider with this but they are out of it,' said Kitty. Two other men sat at the bar and a couple stood by the window. The atmosphere was peaceful and although the surface of the lake was half covered with algae, the sun brightened the water. 'They have dragonflies here,' she said, 'Or they did.'

'And fish in the lake and elves and fairies?' His smile was sweet and teasing and she hoped she could avoid him if he came closer.

'Only when I was a Brownie,' she said. 'Would you like some more beer, Commander?' She rose and put out a hand for his glass. His fingers took her wrist and she was forced to look into his eyes.

'Commander? You did call me Alex just once.' He smiled. 'I do have other names. You have a choice.'

'An imposing string, I believe.'

'If you can bear it, I prefer Alex,' he said. 'It has a lasting quality and grows better the more often it is used. It is good if you have to use it for a long time.' She caught her breath. 'Say it, Kitty.'

'I'll get the beer, Alex,' she said. She tried to make the word banal and flat but the name sounded good, and her voice held a lilt. She knew he was watching her as she went to the bar. He was watching her and wanting her and willing her to understand that he needed her but could not give her his heart. It could blossom into something wonderful if only he would forget Carol. It could dazzle them both and take over their lives and bodies.

She put the mugs on the table again, taking care not to touch him. It would be so easy to look at him and ask if he would like to see her houseboat. A man walked by, and two more people came into the pub.

Alex frowned. 'We ought to go back. I know you have a lot to do, but surely we could have dinner together tonight?'

'I could finish my chores and be ready at eight. Shall I pick you up in my car again? It's not as beautiful as yours but I'm getting to be quite fond of her.'

'Blanche is still using mine, so that would be fine. I want to cram as many interesting things in now as I have to report back on full active duty in three weeks' time. I have official leave when the Surgeon Commander in charge comes back to take over at Osborne and then, back to who knows where?'

'I didn't know it would be so soon.' She felt stricken and fluttered her eyelids down to hide her feelings. He would go away and find his consolation with any of a dozen good looking girls who had no hang-ups about sleeping with attractive men, and perhaps when he was away from Carol her image would fade and another love could enter his life.

'Soon? It's been a damned long time off and on. At times, I thought I'd die of boredom when I was a patient. I wouldn't stay in any one place for long if I had my way. That's why the Service suits me.'

And no hawk could be caged and stopped from flying high, she thought.

'I've learned a lot about true values and about people, Kitty, and I hope I'm a more patient man with those under my care now.' He smiled. 'I've learned that nurses give so much of themselves and understand in a way that doctors could do well to copy.'

'It's all the same profession. You do some things that we can't do and we have skills that a doctor doesn't need.'

'We all need gentle hearts, Kitty.'

'Shall we go?' she said, and went to the powder room to collect her jacket from the bentwood stand. She looked across the room and saw Paul sitting with a man she knew to be a local librarian. She put up a hand to take her jacket from the stand, hoping that she could escape unseen, but behind the bar was a huge pub mirror, bright with the advertising of half a century ago. Beyond the opulent kilt and bonnet worn by the man in the picture extolling the virtues of a famous brand of whisky, Paul saw her reflection and turned.

'Kit, darling! What are you doing here?' He got up from his seat and advanced towards her with both hands outstretched. His eyes were bright with unaccustomed lunch time indulgence in spirits and he seemed very pleased with himself.

'I'm here on duty,' she said. 'The Commander needed ferrying about the Island so I volunteered.' She hoped that the Commander would stay in the men's room for a few more minutes and she hated herself for making excuses for what was a perfectly blameless outing.

'A bit far from base.' He laughed. 'I didn't know the Admiralty had a base at Carisbrooke.' His eyes looked at something beyond her shoulder and she saw Alex walking to the stand to take his jacket.

'Bye for now,' she said.

'He's no patient,' said Paul. 'I doubt if he needs any treatment you could give him unless he includes extras.' His smile was a sneer. 'Nice work to have a pretty nurse everywhere you go, to help whenever necessary.'

'I'm going, Paul,' she said, coldly. 'You have had far too much to drink.'

'When do I see you?' he called after her.

Alex looked back in time to see the man who was calling. He took in every detail of the scruffy shirt and the kind of hair he associated with hippies.

'I don't know,' said Kitty in a clear voice. 'I'll call you sometime, Paul.'

She opened the outer door and held it so that Alex had to follow her. 'You said Paul? Did you expect to meet him here today?'

'I had no idea he would be working here.'

'But this must be his territory and this is where you have all those quaint childhood memories?'

'The Island is a small place. It's like any place where people meet because paths cross.'

One glance told her that he was angry and she could almost think he was jealous. She was furious with herself for being upset and furious with Paul for ruining the delight she had in Alex and their time together. She was also furious with Alex! Why should he take it for granted that any woman would prefer Alex Roscoe to a rather relaxed and amiable man with long hair?

'Some people need a few months in the Service,' he muttered.

'You didn't like Paul?' She smiled, much too sweetly.

'I didn't say that. I don't know him, so I can't

judge, but I imagine you must have a lot in common. You said he did research into place names, family trees, old places?' The way he lingered on each word made it sound as if he compiled something as banal as the mottoes in Christmas crackers.

'He works hard and is becoming quite well known,' said Kitty. 'He would like to move in with me and get married.'

'In that order?'

'No! I mean that we are good friends but each has a separate career. We wouldn't see all that much of each other,' she said, and knew that she sounded as convincing as a damp sponge.

They drove back in near silence and she left him at the entrance to the home. Back at the boat, she tried to convince herself that she could continue with her painting but the paint splashed and she had to scrub the deck and gangway. Alex Roscoe would soon be gone. Couldn't she have had just this one day alone with him? Somehow, Paul had ruined her magic just by being there.

CHAPTER EIGHT

It took a great effort to push the boat clear of the mud and Kitty stopped to get back her breath. It was all very well for Pete to drag it up high and to tie it on a short mooring-rope, but for a girl without his ape-like arms it was difficult to reverse the process. With a sucking noise, the boat gave up the struggle and she could see the rudder half-submerged beneath the cloudy water. It looked all right as far as she could tell, but she would know more when she was afloat and could test the steering.

Her old cord trousers were hot in the afternoon sun and the sweater that covered her warm shirt was loose and overpowering, but she knew that once away from the shore and, if the boat responded in all the right ways, out in the estuary and the sea, she would need all the top covering she possessed. The tiny rowing boat that she used as a tender was tied to the stern and bobbed about like a lamb following its mother. Kitty stepped past it on to the steel ladder of the sailing boat and pulled the loop of rope after her. From the footpath, she heard a shout and saw a man coming towards her houseboat. Damn, she thought. Paul!

She glanced up at the sky and then at the water. If I don't get started now, I shall never manage it today, she thought, and bent to start the engine. To her relief, it burst into activity, drowning the voice that was now quite loud and close. Bad luck, Paul, she thought, with a degree of satisfaction; this is one time when you can't hinder me and have things all your own way. He must have hurried back from Carisbrooke after his working lunch and come straight to her houseboat. The lunch break was not nearly over when she had seen him talking to the man in the pub and they must have had a lot to discuss if they had made a working appointment.

She frowned as the boat cut the water. She had driven back to East Cowes with Alex and then found that she needed one or two more items of shopping when she got home. It had been a mistake to go to the little store run by an old friend who had known the family for years. To think she could escape without at least a twenty minute chat about people she didn't know and would probably never meet, was quite unrealistic, and she had arrived back at the houseboat when the tide was full.

'I haven't much time. Sorry, Paul,' she shouted. 'Tide's turning and I want to test the rudder.' But she could have been whispering. He shouted and she waved in a dismissive way. He would have to wait or call back later. If she was to get down the creek and back before the tide ebbed, she would have to hurry.

The water was slack now and easy to ride, using the engine with no current under the keel, and she let the boat follow the line of the creek along the grassy banks and lush meadows. Behind her the small natural marina fell back and became a picture of flashing paintwork and calm blue water.

For the first time since she had left Alex, she relaxed. The magic of the water soothed her tense spirit and she smiled as the breeze lifted her hair and sent it streaming back from her face in a golden brown wake. She shut her mind to thoughts that might make her unhappy and tried to forget the two men who troubled her in their several ways. Then she saw a man walking the old tow path and caught her breath. It wasn't Alex, but his form was almost as well-set and his hair was dark. If I'm going to see him in every dark-haired man I meet, I shall develop a permanent twitch, she thought wryly.

The breeze strengthened and she hoisted a small sail to see how the boat felt under sail when it heeled over slightly. She held the rudder bar and it all felt good. The engine now seemed unnecessary and she turned it off, revelling in the silence and the taut pull of the wind in the sail. It was going well and her confidence grew. It was no longer important that the tide had turned and she was dependent on the engine if the breeze dropped. The boat responded to the touch on the helm and she crossed the river at a wide sweep and turned into wind. Fine again. She turned back. It was such a lovely afternoon that it was silly to go back now. She stared back towards the houseboat but it was out of sight beyond the curve in the creek. Besides, Paul was there and she had no desire to see him. After drinking spirits, he might be bad-tempered and sarcastic and she had endured enough of chauvinistic men for one day.

The breeze dropped suddenly and the sail flapped. The current was gathering momentum in the middle of the creek as the water rushed towards the sea. The boat turned on the current and Kitty bent to put on the engine again. It sparked and she pulled on the helm. The sail was of no use but she had no hands free to take it in and hoped that the breeze would return. She looked over the side and ths shore was much too close. She pulled at the helm again and the nose of the boat didn't come round nor did the boat change course. The tide was going fast, and mud banks, hidden for the past few hours, now glistened in the sunlight. Kitty cast an agonised glance over the stern and saw what she dreaded. The rudder had sheered away from the pivot pin housing and was trailing limply like a floating shadow on the water.

She recalled the note left by Pete, the man who had made the repair. She might have known that he would take a short cut in his work and use the same old screw holes without making sure they would take the fresh screws. 'She'll do,' he'd said. She certainly will do for me if I'm not quick! thought Kitty. A breeze lifted the sail but the direction had veered. Desperately, Kitty tried to take it down but the current and the sail made the boat turn rapidly towards the mass of grey-brown mud.

Seconds later, the boat was fast, stuck in thick

mud and she knew that it could not be moved until the next tide. 'That's all I need,' she said, crossly. She stowed the sail and made everything fast in case the wind rose. The hatch was locked and she pulled the broken rudder out of the water as the boat lurched to one side on the mud, nearly throwing her off balance, and she wished, not for the first time, that she had a boat with twin keels that would sit primly on mud or sand and not turn to one side. She looked at the thinning stream and sighed. Gingerly she climbed down to the small rowing dinghy and sat in it, pushing away from the yacht with one oar. The mud slid under the flat bottom of the boat and she was able to get to the water, but as she felt the boat flop over the lip of the bank, the other oar in the boat fell astern and joined the merry race of flotsam on its way to Cowes. The boat turned into the race and was swept along with Kitty trying to control it. Somewhere soon, there would be another bend in the creek where an old jetty stuck out into the water. With two oars it would have been easy to row there and to gain land at a place where she could at least telephone for a taxi to take her home, but with one oar she found it difficult even to keep to the side of the creek where the jetty would be.

Grimly, and with aching arms, she used the oar as a paddle, first on one side of the boat and then the other, and her admiration of men who stood nonchalantly in the stern of a small boat using one oar only to ferry across rivers, would have grown, if

she had the time and energy to think of them. The
jetty was in sight and so was a white-painted yacht
that lazily swung on its anchor between her and the
jetty. Kitty let out a very angry, loud and to her ears
a bloodcurdling cry, and knew that collision was
inevitable. She tried to pull the boat away from the
current and made matters worse. The boat came
closer, looming up and showing her that it was
much larger than she had imagined. A head
appeared above the catwalk and a cry answered her
own. 'Hold tight!' he called.

Kitty abandoned the oar and sat low in the boat,
her face in her hands, and waited for the impact.
When it came, she was thrown forward on to her
shoulder, the jutting rowlock stabbing at her upper
arm. The pain was intense and the side of the white
yacht floated in a blur as she closed her eyes,
suddenly nauseated. She lay in the boat and felt it
bucking under her as someone reached for the
painter. A heavy weight joined her in the boat and
strong arms lifted her to a warm hard chest of
someone smelling of salt and maleness and safety.
She felt fingers on her temple, seeking the pulse
and heard a sigh of relief.

Lips that came softly on to her cheek brushed her
lips and her eyelids flickered open. Hazily she
smiled.

'Are you all right?' said Alex Roscoe.

'I think so,' she said and didn't wonder why he
was there. It was wonderful to be held so closely
and to see the expression in those grey-blue eyes

that said, miracle of miracles, that he was worried about her.

'Well, you can climb on board if you are fit,' he said, crisply. 'I'm not giving myself a hernia carrying an able-bodied girl up those steps.'

She blinked. The moment of bliss faded fast. Was he embarrassed to show concern when he kissed her? 'Ouch!' she said as he took away his arm and her shoulder was no longer supported.

He stared. 'Let's get you on board. I'll go first and give you a hand.'

'I can manage. What about your stitches?'

'I have no stitches.'

She clenched her teeth. It was getting quite painful to move her arm. She seized the ladder with her good arm and pulled herself up but she couldn't use the other arm and Alex bent down and supported her while she reached for the next rung. In seconds, she was swung over the rail and on to the soft stern seats on the boat. The hatch was open and he led her down to the cabin where she sank on to a wide and cushioned berth. The dizziness was coming back and she put a hand over her eyes. 'How did you get here?' she said, and passed out.

The next few minutes made no sense. The blur of a man's face came and went through a mist and his voice came from a mountain top. Firm skilled hands removed her sweater and the numb feeling with its core of pain made her shoulder feel three times as big as it should be. The buttons of her shirt were tight, she knew, but Alex was doing very well.

Cold air touched her skin as he drew the good arm out of the sleeve and then pushed the other sleeve away without moving her sore arm. He's a good nurse, she thought and only then realised that he was undressing her. She wondered at his touch on her shoulder. This is madness, she thought in a detached way. How could she lie there calmly and let him disrobe her? She moved away and the pain made her cry out.

'Lie still,' he said, 'I'll try not to hurt you.'

'I'm cold,' she whispered.

'I'll give you something to warm you in a minute,' he said. She moved again, alarmed. She was alone with him on a boat and he was calmly undressing her and saying that!

'I want my shirt,' she said.

'Relax.' But she continued to stare up at him with wide blue eyes. 'Silly girl, you've dislocated your shoulder.'

'I couldn't help it. How was I to know that a boat would be anchored just where I wanted to land?'

But it was impossible to be dignified when she was lying on a bed wearing tight shabby jeans that were very revealing and the only other visible garment was a tiny lace bra that did nothing to hide the swelling curves of her breasts. His hand was on her throat.

'Don't touch me! Go away, my shoulder hurts.'

He gave a sigh of exasperation. 'Before you cry rape, let me explain in words of one syllable! You have, as I said, dislocated your shoulder slightly.

You have two options. You can wait here while I go ashore and ring for an ambulance and that will take time as I shall have to take the boat to a mooring first and find a phone, or you can let me examine it thoroughly and perhaps do something quickly.'

'Oh,' she said in a small voice. 'I'm sorry.'

He grinned. 'Sorry you were obtuse, or sorry no rape?' She blushed and turned her head away. 'I think the pain is less now?' She nodded. It had subsided into a throbbing ache that was almost complete numbness. 'It happens. This the one time it can be reduced while the feeling has gone. It also means that it is treated quickly and has no chance to set like it and make it more difficult to deal with later.' He looked serious. 'Later, you'd have to have an anaesthetic.'

'You aren't going to twist it?'

'You know the score, Kitty. I explained because I now know how one's own judgment can be clouded when we are on the other side of the table and become patients.'

'I do know about that.' She had watched many cases of dislocation dealt with quickly in that way in Casualty. 'But it will hurt?'

'Yes, a little.' He sat back and regarded her with no expression. 'Make up your mind. There isn't a lot of time.' She took a deep breath and nodded. 'Sure?' He sounded as if he now lacked the courage.

'I trust you, Alex,' she said. 'At least, I mean I know you are a good surgeon.'

'Oh, that! You had me worried for a moment. Never trust anyone if you insist on lying around like that.' She blushed with annoyance. 'Good,' he said with approval. 'Blood pressure rising. I'll put on the kettle for coffee. We'll need some soon.' He swung away from her with his new easy movements and she missed his nearness. What if he had tried to make love to her, taking advantage of the fact that she was helpless? From his expression now, the surgeon could well be doing battle with the very sensual man, and the normal desires of a man for a woman in a lonely place.

She braced herself to bear pain, but she bit her lip when he touched her, not for any suffering but for the relentless gentleness of his fingers which bit deeper and deeper into the tissues, finding the seat of the injury. As he had said, the numbness dominated the pain and she felt no great discomfort during the examination. He put a hand under her armpit and smoothed the swollen muscle with the other.

'Good, it's not as bad as I thought. There's no joint damage.' He sounded as if he was giving a lecture to a crowd of students on the ward.

She relaxed. Perhaps he would leave it until later, if it wasn't all that bad. She even smiled, she thought afterwards. She smiled as he calmly jerked her arm and shoulder, sending a searing pain through her body. She screamed and sank back sobbing, an umbrella of pain closing over her, but his hands smoothed the now normal contours of her shoulder and he bent to kiss it.

She wiped away her tears and the numbness was back again. No pain, just the warm sense of release under the lack of sensation. 'You've done it,' she said. 'It's all over!'

'All over? It depends what you mean.'

'I don't have to be a patient and have an anaesthetic.' She moved with infinite caution and she had no pain.

'No, you don't need to go into hospital.' He smiled and then stood up abruptly. 'Coffee, I think.' He went into the galley and left her wondering what he meant. Her hand touched her near-naked breast and she knew how she must appear to him. She reached for her sweater but he came back with a tube of cream that smelled strongly of camphor or the things she associated with athletes and strained muscles.

'You'll need this to take the discomfort of the strained muscles away,' he said. He sat on the edge of the bed and made her turn away slightly. He massaged the cream into her skin. The ache became a blissful warmth, filled with the sensual feeling of firm male hands on her skin. His sure touch brought relief and yet built up an inner tension that threatened to explode. She wanted it to go on for ever, but she wondered if she could take it for another second.

As if he sensed her reaction, he stopped abruptly and went to fetch coffee. He had said nothing while he massaged her shoulder and as he turned away, he drew in his breath, sharply. She struggled into her shirt and when he came back he seemed glad to find her dressed.

She sipped the strong black coffee and shuddered.

'Sorry, no milk, but I didn't expect to stay on board today.'

'It isn't that. You've put brandy in it.'

'I thought we needed it.'

She glanced at his set face. 'You, too? I hope I didn't strain your back when I climbed on board.'

'That was the easy part,' he said. 'Drink up and let's get back to civilisation. I'm fine.'

She sipped the dark brew and watched him over the rim of the mug, wishing that he could let his passion speak, but knowing that she should be grateful for his control. She smiled faintly. Who was she fooling? A girl in pain wouldn't be of much use in bed if that was on his mind. And what of Carol who she had almost forgotten for the past hour? She sipped and the warm spirit flowed down, making everything smoother and easy, and tolerable.

'Why were you anchored here?' she asked at last.

'I thought I'd see if you came this way. I was very unsure if that rudder would stand stress and I knew you would have to float down to the jetty.' He laughed. 'What I didn't expect was to be run down by a wailing banshee.'

'I lost an oar,' she said.

'Oh, Sister Kitty Martin, how could you? I

thought you had everything and everyone under control. I shall treasure the day when I saw you literally up the creek without a paddle.'

'I had one oar,' she said, with dignity. 'I'm not a complete idiot.' She smiled, suddenly, and listened. 'You know this part of the creek?'

He nodded and then his face changed. He hurried on deck and when he came back he saw that she was laughing.

'Well?' she said.

'Damn! Now what do I do?' He looked at her accusingly. 'Did you know that we can't get over that sand bar with a boat of this size?'

'Now who's up the creek?' she said. 'And I thought you had offered me dinner?'

'I'm glad to see that you are better,' he said. 'Well, we have no real choice. There's no food here and we'll have to go to your boat before we eat. You have to change, I hope?'

'There's a telephone a few yards back from the jetty,' she said.

'Good. Your place or mine? We have no real choice. We can't go in opposite directions in one taxi.' He smiled in such a way that Kitty was glad that her heavy sweater was firmly buttoned up, covering her effectively. 'You invited me to tea, remember? We can wait for the tide and I can come back and tow yours up the creek.'

'You can do that tomorrow. I can get someone to fetch mine.'

'Stop gabbling. In another minute, I shall think

that you have a dark secret locked away on that houseboat. Don't you want me to know anything about your private life?'

'Come if you want to,' she said, rudely, to hide her emotion. How could she live on that houseboat once Alex had been there, leaving memories of him lounging on the divan or drinking from her rather good china?

'Such hospitality,' he murmured and took her in his arms. His kiss was nectar and misery. She suspected that he wanted to take her on her own territory, not his own. He would reserve this boat and everywhere he made his for a while for the love that mattered to him. This boat might be Patrick's, but it held memories of Carol sailing with him. He would try to make love to her in a place that was nothing to him and everything to her. She looked at him with misty eyes. Was she never to have more than the crumbs of love?

His eyes mocked her and he laughed, lifting her chin to his lips with one finger. 'Shall we go?' he said and she nodded. 'And Kitty . . . I never make love to women smelling as you do now. That embrocation is stinking the boat. Let's go to your place where you can shower.'

The jetty had been repaired since Kitty landed on it last, and the telephone box was in order. A very amused taxi-driver collected them and tucked away the story of the Surgeon Commander being stranded on a sand bar with a pretty little nursing sister. Kitty wondered just who would hear the exaggerated version tonight in the Sloop. Once again, she was aware of the disadvantages of living in a small community.

Alex viewed the houseboat with interest. 'Very imaginative,' he said, and Kitty felt as if he had handed her a medal.

'Come on board,' she said, forgetting her earlier reservations. 'My turn to make the tea.'

He bent his head to go into the main saloon and looked about him. Sunlight shone through the long window on to the gentle floral covers and the shining woodwork.

'Do you like it?'

'It's charming.' He sat down and leaned against the padded back of the settle. She brought tea and a plate of biscuits and cakes. He shifted his position.

'Are you comfortable?'

'Fine. I wanted to see the room better. You seem remarkably recovered, but wear that scarf as a sling while you sit and rest,' he said.

'It feels wonderful. I doubt if I need it.'

'At least I am now able to see where you live,' he said.

'You didn't sabotage my rudder by any chance?'

'It's a thought. I might have done if I knew what delights there were here for me.' His eyes raked her body and she turned away to the tea tray. 'I shall remember this day for ever, Kitty.'

'I expect you will. It's not every day you get stuck in a boat,' she said, lightly. 'And I was lucky to have a skilled surgeon to rescue me.'

He took the cup she offered and it was overfilled. As the contents slopped on to his shirt, she ran for a towel and hastily mopped up the drips and then scrubbed at the wet patch. Her hair touched his face and he smoothed it against his lips. 'Oh, Kitty,' he whispered, and kissed the hair and her lips and the soft shell of her ear, murmuring soft words that were unintelligible.

'Oh, Hell, what am I doing?' he said. He thrust her away with a groan and she winced. His face was a picture of angry frustration and yet through it came a hint of irrepressible humour. 'Kitty Martin, keep away from me. If you value your body keep away.' He laughed with a touch of hysteria. 'I never thought I'd want anyone smelling as you do now. I shall have to tell the Pharmaceutical Society that embrocation is an aphrodisiac.'

Kitty blushed. 'I'll get that shower,' she said. His kiss had bruised her lips and now he was laughing at her again.

'I want to know about you, Kitty. I haven't a lot of time. I go away soon and I heard on the grapevine that you were leaving Osborne.'

'Next week,' she said. 'I'm taking a break and then deciding what to do.'

'You haven't decided?' He was very still. 'I thought that you might be considering two things. One was marriage to Paul and the other was this?' She was bright pink when she saw the enlistment brochure for the Naval Nursing Service that she had left under a cushion. 'Is this the life you want? To see your husband once in a year or to meet on leave in Australia if you couldn't both get leave in UK? Doesn't he mind having a wife who might be posted anywhere?'

'Carol managed and so do many people.'

'But not you, Kitty.' She looked away. 'You were very ill after the accident in Birmingham,' he said.

'How did you know? And that has nothing to do with my future.'

'I checked. I have my contacts. I wanted to know if you were fit again.' He grinned at the brochure. 'It seems that you are, even if you have a large scar on the left side of your abdomen.'

She put her lips together, and frowned. The nerve of whoever told him! 'I suppose you read my notes.'

'Of course. I suppose you read mine.' He laughed. 'And we know all about our physical records. What are you going to do for love, Kitty?'

'I love my work,' she said. 'We both love our professions, don't we?'

'You no longer mention Paul.'

'I am fond of Paul,' she said. 'But I'm not in love with him. I'm not in love with him as you love Carol.'

'Carol? She is marrying Basil.'

'I know.' She looked up at him with misty eyes. 'It must be terrible for you.' Better to make him admit his love for Carol and so make it clear that she knew that he could offer no more than passion for a moment in time to the nursing sister who had come into his life.

'Carol is wonderful . . . for Basil.' He came close and looked down at her without touching. 'Carol suffered and has got over her grief. My grief was selfish and of another kind.'

She gazed at him in wonder. 'You don't love Carol?'

'Of course I do. Everyone loves Carol but I have no desire to sleep with her or to marry her. We would drive each other nuts in six months.'

'But there was someone? You were saying?'

'Not a woman. When I was wounded, I thought I might not operate again. It was stupid and I was a fool, but I kept thinking. Do you know your Milton? "That one talent . . . lodged with me, useless". Then I came here and found people who had lost so much and I knew I could get back to normal, but it made me rather trying, I believe.'

'You could say that.' She smiled. 'But now you can go back to surgery and a full service life and be happy.'

'That depends. I'm not complete, Kitty. I need someone who will come with me and be there when I need her.'

'I know you . . . fancy me, Alex, but I couldn't just have an affair with you.'

'Because you don't love me?'

She was silent. How could he torture her? Wasn't it evident that she yearned for him with every sensitive fibre of her being? She ached for his kiss on her soft and trembling lips and she wanted him . . . God how she wanted him.

'I suppose you're right.' A tender ripple of laughter echoed in her mind. 'I haven't finished with you. One day, when I was feeling very bloodyminded, I saw a girl chugging up the drive on a most revolting old machine.' Kitty stared and his hands touched her hair. 'I watched and she was wearing the sexiest boots I've ever seen and a helmet that was enough to turn a man's knees to water.' She lowered her glance. He was laughing at her so tenderly that she had to smile. 'She stacked her bike and when she took off the helmet, she had a smear of grease on her cheek.'

'I had to fix the plug,' she said.

'I was so used to immaculate women in starched dresses and stiff hair under service hats, that I wanted to kiss away that oil and I've wanted to kiss away all her hang-ups and self-deception ever since.'

She tried to laugh. 'I said . . . you fancied me.'

'How can you let that phrase pass your lips? You talk too much, woman.' He kissed her. 'I shall have to stop you talking if you say such silly things.'

He kissed her again and her hands stole round his neck like small kittens, soft and timorous. The power of his love began to dawn.

'Don't you see how much I love you, you little fool? Don't you see that I shall never be complete without you? I can never be complete until I can wake in the morning with my love beside me, her hair across the pillow and her sweet tender breasts under my hand.'

She shuddered with the growing force of her own joy. His arms were about her, crushing her softness and as he caressed her back and thighs, her body seemed to dissolve to his shape and they swayed together in the fierce gentleness of knowing.

'And will your love last?' she asked.

'Would a lifetime be enough?' he said. He held her close, with tenderness rather than urgency. 'We have to make plans,' he said. 'Blanche is already seeing all those naval uniforms and crossed swords for a double wedding, but we can't tell her anything until you have got rid of that unholy smell. I can't ruin our first night together with a memory like that. But make it soon, Kitty, or it will be no use protecting your virtue with embrocation.'

She fled to change and knew that he could never ruin the ambience of her home by the river. It would be a haven for them when they returned from their wanderings.